# THE GORDONSTON LADIES DOG WALKING CLUB UNLEASHED

(THE GORDONSTON LADIES DOG WALKING CLUB PART II)

By
DUNCAN WHITEHEAD

**Fiction Statement**

**As always, for Keira**

# CHAPTER ONE

His body was much heavier than she had anticipated. It had taken her twenty minutes to remove the sheet-wrapped corpse from the trunk of her car and drag it from the street, through the gate that led to the rear of her house and then along the path leading to her back yard. She wiped her brow as trickles of sweat began to pour from her forehead.

She checked the time once more on her watch; it was 4 am. It appeared that no one had seen her, but she had remained vigilant, checking for the twitching of curtains, passing vehicles and any early morning dog walkers or returning late night revelers - she was satisfied that her nocturnal activities were not being watched. The last thing she needed was a curious neighbor or passerby witnessing her dragging a sheet-wrapped body from the rear of her new SUV. She paused for breath, sweat now pouring from her brow, which she again wiped away, leaving a trail of dirt across her forehead, dirt from the hole she had dug the previous evening in her back yard. A hole that had taken her hours to dig and a hole that was soon to become a grave.

It had taken her over three hours to dig the grave, again while ensuring she was not seen, and she had had to destroy many of the plants and flowers it had taken her years to grow, but it was a necessary consequence of burying a body, and there was simply nowhere else viable for such an endeavor. She sighed as she stared at the pile of disrupted flowers and plants. Her butterfly weeds and the hibiscus they'd planted when they had first moved into their home had been totally destroyed.

She smiled to herself. He had hated gardening. Detested it. She had lost count of the times they had argued and fought over her flower garden and plants. He had wanted to grow vegetables, to save money for one thing, but she saw no beauty in onions and potatoes. She had allowed him to plant a tomato bush, which remained intact and undamaged by the digging. Wherever he was, he would probably be laughing that her gardening labor of love had had to make way for a grave. Ironic, she thought, replacing the living for the dead.

Eventually, after what had seemed an eternity, she stood over the hole; it looked deep enough; four feet deep had been her aim. Though she wasn't an expert, she estimated that her digging had been sufficient. She stood about five feet and four inches tall, so she guessed if she stood in the grave then she could estimate the depth. The last thing she needed were wild animals digging up the body; the thought of a neighborhood dog, or even cat, running around with bones in their mouths sent shivers down her spine. She jumped into the hole and her head peered over the top. Yes, she was confident it was deep enough.

The corpse, which was securely wrapped in the bed sheet, lay at her feet. For a minute she just stared at it. She had expected to feel more than she did, more grief, more sorrow, but the truth was that she felt relieved more than anything. She was glad it was eventually over. The hard part was done, mentally and emotionally anyway; the physical hardships, compared to what she had done earlier that day, were easy.

She bent over, and placed a hand on the body. Despite her indifferent feelings of grief, a solitary tear fell from her eye. Intermingled with her sweat and the soil on her face, it formed a dark stain on the once pristine clean white sheet.

She looked backwards, towards her home. It was dark and silent, and the building's sole occupant had been sleeping for hours. She thought about praying but dismissed the idea as pointless and hypocritical. She wasn't even religious, and he certainly hadn't been. There was, though, one more thing she had to do. She entered the shed that sat to the right of the destroyed plant bed and the freshly dug grave, and retrieved the bag of lime salts that had sat there for weeks. She understood that these lime salts would assist with the decomposition of the corpse and help mask any smell produced as a result of the decomposition. He had told her that.

"I guess I will miss you," she whispered. "I know *she* will miss you," she added. She placed her hand on the sheet, one final gesture of affection, though even that seemed forced and contrived. Would she really miss him? She wasn't even sure. One thing was sure, her life would be easier without him.

With all the strength she could muster she rolled the body into the hole and watched as it tumbled into its final resting place. She sighed and took a deep breath. It was done. She lifted the half full bag of lime salts and scattered the contents into the grave, covering the sheeted corpse. Glancing to her left she picked up the same shovel she had used earlier that evening to dig the grave and began filling in the hole; shoveling the earth back to where it had come from. It was far easier, she thought, filling a grave than digging one, something else he had been right about. She paused for a moment. How many times had he done this? How many graves had he dug? How many families grieved and mourned for loved ones, with no knowledge where their bodies lay?

In the morning she would plant more flowers and maybe even vegetables; to cover the grave and to help disguise the unevenness of her disturbed garden. In a few weeks no one would ever even guess her flowerbed had been disrupted and hidden below it, a dead body. Not that she had many visitors anyway, and those she did have she doubted paid much attention to her gardening efforts. He certainly hadn't.

So it was done. He was gone. Their lives would be so different now and she knew that *she* would miss him, and the truth was, sadly, that *she* would be the only one to miss him, and maybe even the only person to notice he was no longer around. Briefly, that thought filled her with fleeting sadness, not for him, but for *her,* but, as time would pass, he would become just a memory, and then *she* would move on. Kids were like that. They had no real concept of death, not at her age at least, there were more important things to think about, such as toys and games.

Thirty minutes later the hole was covered and filled. It had been a long and tiring night; in fact the whole day had been tiring. She was exhausted. She could not recall the last time she had felt so tired, so drained. She yearned for her bed, the bed she no longer shared, and the sleep she so desperately needed.

Suddenly she heard a sound behind her. She turned her head quickly and instinctively dropped the shovel. It was the sliding door opening, the sliding door leading from the den to her back yard.

"Honey, get back to bed. You shouldn't be wandering around," said Veronica Partridge as she abandoned her task, though sufficiently completed in any case.

"Mommy, I was having a bad dream," explained Katie Partridge turning back to enter the house as her mother followed behind her.

"Well, mommy is here now, so we can forget all about bad dreams. Where is bunny?"

Katie raised her left hand and produced a small stuffed rabbit. "Here he is, mommy, I have him," she replied.

"Well," said Veronica Partridge, as she collected her

daughter in her arms, not caring about the dirt and sweat that covered her body, "that's all that matters."

Katie Partridge giggled and lifted her stuffed toy into the air, showing her mother that bunny was indeed safe in her custody, then her face took a more serious look. "Mommy, I have a question," she said.

"Sure, honey, what is it?" replied Veronica Partridge as she slid the back door shut, taking one last glance at the recently dug grave.

"Where's Daddy?"

# CHAPTER TWO

"Poor Kelly. You know she has been staying with her parents for the past few months, and did you know that her garden is looking simply awful? I dread to think what the inside of the house is like. Filthy no doubt, probably full of roaches. I can only imagine the smell, totally abandoned. It's so very sad. "

"I heard she was going to sell the house, or at least was trying to, but can't until she gets a signature from Tom. I still can't get over the fact that he left her like that. In fact, I heard the house was already in foreclosure. She simply isn't paying the mortgage, probably can't afford it. The poor girl. I seriously doubt she will ever return. And who can blame her? I believe she left everything. All the furniture is still in the house, all their possessions still in the closets, her beautiful clothes, those fancy shoes she used to wear and no doubt a ton of makeup. I would suppose his things are still there, too. He didn't take a thing. Yes, I heard it was just abandoned as well, a bit like her, the poor dear."

"Some men are like that. Simply never satisfied with what they have, always wanting more, always on the lookout for someone 'better'," said Carla Zipp, just before she took a mouthful of her gin and tonic, disguised, as always, in a red disposable plastic cup. "Such a shame for the poor girl. And to think we all thought Tom was such a saint. It just shows that we really have no idea what people are really like, neighbors, friends - present company excepted - mainly men though, you just can't rely on them."

Her two companions nodded their agreement and also proceeded to take a sip of their preferred alcoholic beverages from their respective plastic cups.

The Gordonston Ladies Dog Walking Club, as they had done for the last four months, devoted much of their conversation to the topic of Kelly and Tom Hudd. As far as they had concluded, Tom had left his beautiful wife Kelly four months previously; just got up one morning and vanished. No note, no explanation, just disappeared off the face of the earth. Initially he had been reported as a missing person by Kelly, but after a few weeks the police stopped searching for Tom. Kelly, it was rumored, was convinced Tom had left her, for what reason no one knew, and subsequently the police had taken the same view. There had never been a real search for him; he was just one of the countless thousands of people who go missing every year, leaving no trace as to their whereabouts nor reason for their running away. The only mystery had been poor Shmitty, the Hudd's Labrador, who Tom had been supposedly walking that morning in the very park where the women now sat. The poor dog had been sitting on his owner's porch, just waiting for someone to open the front door to let him in, his leash still attached to his collar, and, according to rumors, crying and yelping, until Kelly had opened the door, disheveled and obviously confused. Cindy, the Hudd's neighbor, had pointed out that Kelly had been sick the week Tom had gone missing, some virus or bug she had picked up in France, during the vacation she had won.

Heidi Launer shook her head. "What with Tom leaving Kelly and that scruffy lazy Englishman abandoning his wife and child, poor Veronica, let's not forget her, this neighborhood has had its fair share of nasty characters, in my opinion, present company, of course, excepted."

Heidi's companions nodded their agreement.

"How could anyone abandon a child? asked Cindy Mopper. "She is such a cutie. Thank the Lord she looks more like her mother than him. I can't say I will miss him, never liked him in the first place. I am sure he was another one who never scooped up his dog's poop. Good riddance to bad rubbish, that's what I say."

Both Heidi and Carla agreed with their fellow dog walker. Both Veronica and Kelly were very attractive women, and they were all positive that sooner or later they would meet decent men, men who wouldn't simply leave them, for whatever the reason. The general consensus around the picnic table where the women sat and drank their cocktails was that most men were inherently evil, not all men though.

"Thank heavens for decent men, hardworking honest men, who would never dream of hurting anyone, let alone children and women. Thank the Lord for the few who make up for the bad ones, like Elliott for example," said Cindy Mopper as she took another swig of booze, the ice clinking as she raised her plastic cup to her lips, "and of course my Billy. Did I mention Billy is coming back to Gordonston tomorrow?" she asked her friends. She had, of course, many times, but her two friends smiled and nodded politely as if this was fresh and new news.

"You are lucky to have Billy," said Carla as she gently touched her friend's hand. "The things you tell me about him do go to prove that there is some goodness out there. All he does for those poor children, all he does for charity, you must be so proud of him."

Cindy indicated that she was indeed extremely proud of him, and the fact that he was positively the exact opposite of most men. He was honest, kind, selfless and, as she often said, a true saint.

As the women sat at their usual spot, the picnic table adjacent to the Scout Hut in Gordonston park, their three dogs, Fuchsl, Paddy and Walter played together as they had done for the past five years. Though not as sprightly as they once were, the dogs still made the most of the wooded area and spacious outdoor park which they frequented. It was their domain. As the park was strictly reserved for residents, it was very rare that any outsider would ever venture into the park; the signs displayed on both gates to the park, warning that it was indeed for the residents of Gordonston only, a facility just for them, and that violators would be reported to the police. Each one of the three women, who sat drinking their cocktails and gossiping, had at least on four occasions called 911 after spotting non-authorized persons either walking their dogs in their park, or children from outside the neighborhood playing on the wooden swings, slide and climbing frame.

"Elliott is certainly going to win," said Cindy with a smile, changing the subject, as she glanced over towards the large white house that overlooked the east side of Gordonston Park. "The election is just a week away and apparently he is well ahead in the polls. He is going to make such a fantastic Mayor. I just know it."

Carla nodded her agreement, while Heidi, unnoticed by her companions, took an extra-large swallow of her gin and tonic.

"He has my vote, that's for sure," said Carla. "I hear that you have been doing a bit of canvassing for the good cause?" Her question directed at Cindy.

"Yes, I have. I have delivered flyers, attended functions and offered him my full assistance. It is, I am sure, what Thelma would have wanted. If only she were alive today, she would be so proud of him. Like we all are," replied Cindy.

Once again Heidi did not comment, instead she took an even larger swig of her cocktail.

"Well, good for you," smiled Carla. "You know, I really do think you two would make a great couple. I think Thelma would have loved that, for you and Elliott to maybe 'hook up'. I really wish you would. I think a powerful man like Elliott Miller needs a strong woman behind him. You could be the 'First Lady' of Savannah."

A few months ago, a comment like that from Carla would have had Cindy seething, but now, things had changed. Carla had made it perfectly clear to Cindy, and anyone else who cared to listen, that she preferred her men younger. And why not? The woman was spectacular; she looked half her age, and of course, she knew it.

Cindy waved away her friend's last statement. "I am sure he is just far too busy right now to even consider any sort of relationship. Even though I do agree. I am sure that is what Thelma would have wanted, but, well, one can only hope!"

Carla and Cindy both laughed. However, once again, Heidi remained stern and passed no comment while she took her third rather large swig of gin and tonic.

"So what did happen to Veronica's husband?" asked Carla. "I don't think I ever spoke to him, always thought he was strange. Did he go back to Australia?"

"I thought he was English?" interrupted Heidi.

"Australian, English, British… it's all the same really," Carla continued.

"Well," said Cindy, "I heard he got a job. Somewhere abroad, not sure where, he just packed his bags and flew away, leaving poor Veronica and that beautiful little girl all alone. He hasn't been back. Not sure if they are even still together, but Veronica seems to be fine. She has that brand new car, and I see there has been a lot of work done on their house. I also heard she has stopped working, so he must be doing well; he was some sort of accountant, I believe. Anyway, can't say I miss him, rude man, Unlike Tom, you know he was a fantastic boy. I have no idea why he would leave Kelly."

As it usually did, the women's gossiping went full circle. They repeated previously made statements and comments, disregarding the fact that one of the trio had already uttered the exact same words. It was always the same, maybe a result of the alcohol, and minds not as young as they once were. It was only Heidi, who was actually the eldest of the three, who remained on point, who never repeated herself. It was a mild annoyance to her that her two friends virtually repeated the same thing, day in day out; it really irked her. She found it tedious, but, she supposed, what else did they have, apart from gossip and their dogs? At least she had a purpose, something to aim for.... She stared at Elliott Miller's house and finished her drink.

It was now Carla's turn to take a large sip of her cocktail. Turning her head, she called for her bulldog, Walter, who was busy exploring the northwest corner of the park, sniffing and scratching at the earth. "Walter, stop that!" shouted Carla. Walter immediately stopped his exploring and excavating and returned to play with his canine friends. Unnoticed by her friends, Carla shivered, she knew that Tom Hudd was likely buried somewhere in the park. Though she had no idea who had killed him, she presumed, correctly, that whoever had killed Tom on her behalf had done so in the park, and probably buried him here also. The last thing she wanted was for her continually digging Walter to run back to the table with a part of his body. The mere image of one of the dogs running around with a human arm or a leg bone in their mouths filled her with dread. She was thankful that Tom was regarded as a missing person, and had been delighted to hear that the police did not suspect any foul play. The consequences, if Tom's body were ever discovered, could potentially be disastrous; an investigation could lead back to her. Gino, her unrequited love in Las Vegas, who had orchestrated, on her behalf, Tom's demise, had assured her that there would be no trace back to her, that the 'Organization' who had carried out Tom's murder were the best and had protocols in place, ensuring that 'clients' remained protected. Still, though, she worried, and of course, despite her readiness to have a man killed, she didn't have the stomach to see the aftermath. She was, of course, a lady.

"Maybe he had another woman," said Carla coyly as she placed her cup on the picnic table. "Maybe he even had a secret lover," she added, staring into space.

"Oh, I doubt it," said Cindy. "They were such a perfect couple, but, you know, stranger things have happened. But please, let's be realistic here, I don't know any woman as gorgeous as Kelly. I mean, it's not as if there is an abundance of women around here who could even compete with Kelly."

Carla, once again unnoticed by her companions, smirked. If only you knew, she thought, if only you knew.

"Well, I heard, what's his name, Doug? I heard that Veronica has no idea where he is. That all this talk of a fancy new job is nothing but hearsay, gossip and rumor. I do wish people around here wouldn't do that. Gossip that is. It is how rumors start. It's hard to work out what is fact and fiction." The irony of Carla's last statement was missed by her friends. Considering that they were the root of all the neighborhood gossip and created more rumors, regardless of fact, was beyond their comprehension.

"He probably ran off with a floozy," added Heidi, reluctantly joining in with the revolving conversation surrounding the antics of Tom Hudd and Doug Partridge. "I bet they both had fancy women, and I bet that's where they are. Shirking responsibility and having fun at the expense of their poor wives. Let's face it — it is the only plausible scenario."

Carla and Cindy, as they often did, concurred with their older friend. They continued talking together, recounting stories about other men who had run off with fancy women, floozies and such like.

Heidi Launer wasn't listening to her friends. She was looking in the direction of Elliott's house, her face twisted, almost into a sneer. She tightened her grip on her now empty plastic cup, almost crushing it. How the hell was the man still breathing? She had paid the required money requested. Her son Stephen had assured her that Elliott would be taken care of, but no, he was still here, now likely to become Mayor. It was just wrong. The man was a liar and a fraud and he had hoodwinked the whole of Savannah. Heidi, though, knew different. His speeches, his kissing of babies, his promises of building a better Savannah meant nothing to her. He was one of *them*, *they* were greedy, *they* lied, *they* manipulated and *they* stole. *They* plagiarized.

"Are you all right, Heidi?" asked Carla, who had noticed the stern expression on the elderly woman's face.

"Yes, yes I am fine," said Heidi, her scowl quickly disappearing, and a smile forming on her face. "I was miles away… miles away. Just thinking about Thelma and the fun we used to have. You know me, very sentimental and always living in the past."

The trio of ladies smiled in unison and once more took swigs from their beverages. The conversation then turned to Thelma Miller, the founding member of The Gordonston Ladies Dog Walking Club. Each woman had a different, yet highly amusing story regarding their departed friend. Cindy recalled the time that Thelma had, during an afternoon cocktail drinking and dog walking session in the park, climbed a tree. Getting up had been no problem; it was getting down that had caused the hilarity. Drunk and slurring her words, she had demanded that someone fetch a trampoline so she could jump down. Of course, there was no trampoline. In the end it had been Cindy who had fetched a ladder from Thelma's garage so she could climb down from the tree.

Carla giggled as she reminisced about the time Thelma had been so sloshed that she had fallen asleep on the picnic table. Despite everyone's efforts to waken her she had not stirred, continued snoring, and at one stage passed wind as she slept. The women had had to call Elliott to come and fetch his wife. Carla laughed out loud at the image of Elliott carrying Thelma home. Of course it had not just been the drink. It was her medication, so Thelma often explained, that made her unable to recall any event involving her and the fun it gave her friends.

Heidi also smiled. There was the time Thelma, while being treated with chemotherapy for her cancer, had spotted two strangers in the park, two nonresidents of Gordonston, just taking a stroll through the wooded area. She had confronted them, told them to leave, and just to make sure they knew she was serious, she had removed her wig, warning them that the park was full of bugs, that if they got into a person's hair, they ate it. Heidi laughed as she remembered the two encroachers running as fast they could out of the park.

"Oh, I nearly forgot," said Cindy excitedly. "The house on Henry Street, the Carter's old house – well they finally got it rented out. You know they are moving to Canada? Well, they didn't want to sell, but they didn't want the place empty, so they found a nice old man who signed a short term contract. They left their furniture, so they wanted someone mature; apparently he is perfect. I hear that he is a very polite gentleman, quite old I believe, extremely polite; that's what Brenda Carter said anyway."

Carla and Heidi nodded their agreement. It was important, they concurred, when renting your home, and leaving your own furniture in the place, that you select a tenant who is going to respect your possessions.

Cindy continued, "He is a single man, widower she, Brenda Carter, said, 'foreigner'. She wasn't sure from where. You know Brenda, she's not as good as we are at getting information, or even getting her facts right. European though, she knows that. Poland? Hungary? One of *those* places she said, who knows where. But definitely from Eastern Europe. Was it Rumania? I don't know. Anyway, he moves in tomorrow, just for a couple of months. Brenda said he was a lovely little Jewish man, who won't bother anyone. I told her that is just what Gordonston needs. Nice people who keep their business to themselves. Peace and quiet; there's been too much drama lately."

Carla and Heidi nodded that they agreed with their friend. Gordonston was a genteel neighborhood. No riff raff. He sounded an ideal neighbor. Once again though, another scowl crossed Heidi's face, again unnoticed by her friends, and once again she tightened her grip on the empty plastic cup.

"Well, I hope this newcomer abides by the rules of the park. Does he have a dog?" asked Heidi, loosening her grip on the now totally crushed cup.

"Apparently not," replied Cindy. "In fact I don't really know *too* much about him. But Brenda did say that they would not be entertaining pets. She had stipulated quite clearly in the rental agreement that no tenant could bring pets. Of course I agree. You can't have someone bringing cats and dogs into someone else's furnished home. They would scratch the furniture. No, no dog."

"That's a relief," said Heidi. "The last thing we need is another old man walking around not scooping. We have enough of them already. 'You know who' for a start, but I am happy to report that Mr. Jackson has not been frequenting the park recently. So it seems he may have taken notice of our letters."

Cindy and Carla once again sycophantically agreed with Heidi.

"Good," said Cindy, "I will drink to that." She raised her cup to her lips and finished the last drops of her cocktail. "I mean, there is a scooper provided. Some people just have no respect for others. I for one am glad he has not been around lately. Horrible old man."

"What sort of name is Ignatius anyway?" asked Carla. "If you ask me, we should take it further. Actually try and get him banned from the park." Carla then proceeded to finish her drink.

"Well, time for me to get home," said Heidi. "Betty

Jackson is making Brunswick stew, and Fuchsl looks tired. Same time tomorrow, ladies?" she asked as she rose from the table.

"Wouldn't miss it for the world," replied Cindy, also rising from the picnic table.

"Count me in," said Carla as she stood.

The women called their dogs, who bounded towards them and followed the trio of ladies as they left the park, leaving three empty red plastic cups strewn on the picnic table, one of them crushed, an empty trash can only yards from the table next to the unused, but much needed, pooper scooper.

# CHAPTER THREE

Ignatius Jackson coughed into his handkerchief and, not for the first time that morning, groaned in pain and then stared at the blood stained cloth. He knew he did not have long to live. Days had now been replaced by hours, and the weakness that engulfed this once fit man belayed the strength of his mind and his memories. Chalky, his Cairn terrier, whimpered as Ignatius tried to rise but fell back onto his bed, unable to muster the strength needed to even pet his best friend.

"Not long now, Chalky," whispered the frail old man. "Not long now I think, old friend. You go outside, boy. I left the back door open, so you can just wander outside and do your business." Chalky did not move. He stared at his master, his head cocked to the left, before he lowered his body and returned to lie at the side of his owner's bed.

Ignatius smiled. Chalky wouldn't leave his side. He had never questioned the phrase 'man's best friend' – as without doubt, this small dog was his best friend. Loyal and obedient, just like Ignatius in a way, he thought, honorable even. But that was where the similarity between man and dog ended.

Ignatius did not consider himself honorable — far from it.

"Look at you," he said again, "not leaving my deathbed, waiting for me to get better. I am sorry to say, old friend, I don't think I will be getting any better. Don't you worry though, I have made sure you are going to be fine, just fine." Deathbed. It was an odd phrase thought, Ignatius, it was just still a bed after all. One could not purchase a deathbed, not that he was aware of anyway. Maybe he should have gone into another business. Maybe, when he left the army he should have sold deathbeds, so there would be no confusion as to which bed a person should die in. He smiled again at his notion. At least he still had some sense of humor, despite the agony of the cancer ravaging his body. At least his mind was still working.

Ignatius had always planned ahead, partly due to his military background. 'Piss poor planning promotes piss poor performance' had been one of his favorite sayings to his men. It always got laughs, but it was deadly serious, and it was still a code that Ignatius lived by, and, soon, he was sure, would die by. He had spoken to the pastor of his church and told him that if he hadn't called him by Sunday, which was five days away, to come to the house, where the back door would be ajar, and to take Chalky for a few days. A friend of Ignatius would then collect the dog and provide him with a new home. Ignatius just hoped the pastor understood what he meant. He wanted no fuss and had made it clear that he wanted to die in peace and alone, except for Chalky. He wasn't sure if the pastor had taken him seriously, and Ignatius, who never relied on anyone, wasn't even sure if he could rely on his pastor. Anyway, he thought, he was sure it would be fine. Chalky was just as self-sufficient as his master was. Ignatius, before he had become bedridden, had opened up a large bag of dried food, enough food to feed Chalky for months, but no doubt it was now all scattered about the kitchen floor. He had also filled over fifty large bowls with water, enough to quench his friend's thirst for weeks. No, Chalky would not starve, nor would he become dehydrated, in the event no one followed his instructions.

Ignatius had not left his bed for two days. His only forays were to the bathroom, an endeavor that caused even more pain and an abhorrent amount of time. He was a proud man, though, he would not dirty his sheets, and it was, of course, a matter of honor. Honor. That word again. What was honorable about dying alone in a bed? Where was the honor in that? Where was the honor in marking people for death? Where was the honor sitting behind a desk, instructing others to kill? The army had been different. He had had honor then. Not now. He had let anger, vengeance and greed dictate his twilight years. She would not have been proud of him, he knew that. She would have stopped him; she would not have condoned his second career. Ignatius sucked in air. He would not cry, he would not shed a tear for himself, his life and his chosen path. No, he may not have honor, but he had pride and he had integrity, and he felt sorry for no man, let alone himself.

Ignatius Jackson had no fear of death. He had been surrounded by it all his life. Vietnam, Korea and other 'operations' that many knew nothing about. And then of course there was the 'Organization'; dealers in death, and he had been a pivotal cog in the never ending machine of killing. His only concern now was for Chalky, and of course, the child. He had done all he could, and he hoped that no harm would come to the child. She was innocent, she was pure, and though he had no pity for others, he pitied the innocent.

All Ignatius had now was his memories. Memories that to a degree relieved his suffering, memories that were still fresh in his mind. Memories that no one, not the 'Organization', not even cancer could take away. He closed his eyes and his mind drifted, taking him back, taking him back to another time, another place, another life….

* * * * *

"You are not on the base anymore, you do know that?

You do realize that this is meant to be a time of rest and recreation. For the good Lord's sake, rest man," said May Jackson as she sat at her dresser combing her hair. "You know you don't have to get up at six in the morning every day, there are no men to inspect, guns to clean, or whatever it is you boys do?" She smiled into the mirror and turned to face her husband. Ignatius Jackson smiled back.

They had been man and wife for twelve months, and had married two days after Ignatius had returned from the war. For the past six months he had been based at Hunter Army Airfield in Savannah, and the highly decorated Colonel and his new bride had recently found the perfect home to raise a family. Sure, it was big, too big. May often commented that they should have bought a smaller home, but they had both fallen in love with not only the house, but the neighborhood. Gordonston was ideal. The park, which their home overlooked, would be a perfect place for their planned children to play. They could watch them from the room in the turret that gave them a perfect view of the park, unobstructed by trees or bushes. They would even get a dog, a big dog, whom the children, when they came, would love and play with. They would spend many happy afternoons in the park, they were sure; children, a dog, maybe even a cat.

"I can't help it," replied Ignatius. "It is a habit, and anyway, I feel guilty taking this leave while you have to go to work. I want to wake up with you so I can spend as much time as possible in your company, if you will permit me, ma'am?"

May laughed. She certainly did not mind. She had married the man of her dreams. Handsome, strong, kind and a hero. Not only that, but two years ago, in 1975, at the young age of 30, her fiancé; now her husband, had become the youngest Colonel in the US Army and the first African American in his battalion's history to attain the rank. Life was good. In a few months Ignatius would be transferred to Fort Benning, where he would take command of the US Army sniper school. As one of the military's most highly accomplished and decorated snipers, it had been a dream post, and May, though a little perturbed that she would only see her husband at weekends and during his leave periods, was proud of him. It was a small sacrifice, and anyway, they had their whole lives ahead of them. And of course, she couldn't leave her job. She wouldn't. She loved it, and there was no way she was going to waste all those months of nursing college just to sit around being the Colonel's wife. She was constantly amazed at those women, the other wives of the senior officers, who spent their days drinking tea and coffee, chit chatting about nothing in particular; it would drive her mad. Of course Ignatius was in full agreement. He knew his wife was a strong willed woman, so even if he did insist she accompany him on his posting, he knew that he would be wasting his time.

"So, how are you going to spend the day, sweetheart?" asked May as she continued combing her hair, watching her husband dress, his body reflected in the mirror.

"I am not sure," replied Ignatius, "maybe prepare you a nice dinner. Read the newspaper, maybe wash the car. I only have seven days of leave remaining – to be honest, I can't wait to get back. I miss my boys."

May rose from the dresser, her crisp white nurses' uniform emphasizing her elegant figure and beauty. "Your boys, your boys…I hope your boys realize how lucky they are to have a boss like you," she said smiling. She walked over to her husband, hugged his muscular torso, and ran her finger down his well-toned and defined arm and kissed him on the lips.

"You can forget about spending the day reading the newspaper, or cleaning the car for that matter… we have a new house! There are boxes that still need unpacking, the den could use a lick of paint and don't forget the garden. Only seven days? I expect this house to be perfect in five," she laughed.

Of course she was right, thought Ignatius, there were many jobs to do around the house. Yes, the den needed painting, and he still hadn't unpacked all the moving boxes. He wanted to hang his decoration medals, and he had decided the wall by the stairs would be perfect. He hated gardening, but of course, like a good soldier, and even better husband, he would obey his wife's orders. Maybe he would even paint the room they had earmarked as a nursery, so it would be ready when, well when they were ready. Which Ignatius hoped would be soon.

"I love you, Colonel Jackson," said May, staring into her husband's eyes.

"I love you, Nurse Jackson, more," he replied.

"That's impossible," replied May.

"Are you sure I can't drive you to the hospital? I really don't mind," offered Ignatius.

May had begun working at Savannah's Memorial Hospital only three weeks previously. Already she had made friends and was popular amongst her new colleagues. Dedicated, hardworking, but above all caring, it had already been tipped she would soon be a candidate for early promotion.

"No, Margaret is going to drive me. I am going to walk to her house; it is only a block away; she likes to gossip before we start our shift. I kind of enjoy listening to her stories and gossip to be honest. I guess sooner or later though, you are going to have to teach me to drive."

Ignatius agreed. With him soon to be posted to Fort Benning he would have to ensure his wife was as self-sufficient as she could be. He promised that this weekend he would begin giving her driving lessons, and once she had obtained her license he would buy her a car.

Ignatius grinned and kissed his wife again. He had never expected life could be this be good, this perfect, and it could only get better. They had promised to wait two more years before starting a family. As May was eight years younger than

Ignatius, they had time. During the war, the thought of marrying and spending his life with May had been the one thing that had got him through the horrors of battle and the stress of command. The thought of raising a family, living comfortably and watching his children grow, eventually having kids of their own and growing old with May at his side had spurred him in the heat of battle. He had survived much, and it was his determination to live a long and happy family life that had kept him focused and alert.

"I will see you tonight," said May as she exited the bedroom. "I love you."

"And I love you."

* * * * *

Ignatius Jackson coughed again and sighed, after all these years the memories seemed so fresh. That day, that happy day, had remained in his memory as if it was only yesterday - moving into their new home, painting the nursery, planning for their life together. His marriage had been perfect, but children had never come. His dream of becoming a father had never come true. The nursery never was used, and the sound of their home had never been filled with children's laughter, toys, cats and a big dog. May could not have children; twice she had suffered miscarriages which devastated both of them. They had considered adoption, but with her career, and his, they simply didn't think it would be fair.

Chalky looked up to his master, as he groaned in pain once more. At the age of forty, he had retired from the army, a result of cut backs. Initially he had struggled with adjusting to civilian life, though he received a very generous pension, and with May's salary, who had now become a senior nurse, they were financially comfortable. After two months of sitting at home, gardening, which he still hated, cooking and being the proverbial house husband, he had taken a second career.

He obtained a degree in teaching, a vocation that his wife encouraged, and he had spent the next twenty years of his life as a high school teacher. He remembered fondly the children he had taught; he was proud of them all. Many had joined the military; their decisions based on his advice. He was seen as a caring and dedicated educator, popular not only with the pupils, but his fellow teachers also. He was respected and admired by parents, held in high regard by the Board of Education, and it was predicted that one day he would become principal.

But then came the sickness. Gradually his health began deteriorating; initially it was mild aches and pains, the odd unexplained bout of tiredness. The day he had collapsed, while teaching a class, had been his final day as a teacher. Tests were conducted, results waited on, and, when eventually he was diagnosed with cancer, it had been May who had proven to be his rock. She insisted on a regime of vitamins and healthy eating, coupled with his prescribed medication, and due to the treatment he received the cancer, while never cured, did not spread as expected. Defying his doctors, Ignatius lived, lived well, and though his physicians had given him a prognosis of living only for a few more years, he had survived.

Though they could never be sure, both Ignatius and May were convinced his sickness was a result of the chemicals and various agents and gasses he had come into contact with during his military service. Ignatius harbored the notion that his contact with Agent Orange, which the **U.S. military,** as part of its **herbicidal warfare** program, **Operation Ranch Hand**, had used during the Vietnam War, an Operation Ignatius had been involved in, had caused his cancer.

Ignatius had been told, as had his fellow soldiers, while in Vietnam, not to worry, and was persuaded the chemical was harmless. Of course, it hadn't been. Ignatius also suspected that it was his exposure to Agent Orange that had led to his wife's miscarriages. Unlike many, who had tried and failed to seek compensation and disability payments, and extra health care, for conditions they believed were associated with exposure to Agent Orange, Ignatius hadn't even bothered to make a claim.

Despite the knowledge that sooner or later he would eventually succumb to the cancer, that one day the disease would spread, he made the most of his life, brushing aside his illness, and dealing with life as he always had, with dignity, strength and courage. He had volunteered at the local church, which was located in Gordonston, Christ's Community Church, located along Kinzie Avenue. He would spend most of his day there, not only volunteering for church projects, but counseling and providing advice and guidance to all who sought it. He was pivotal in fund raising efforts and organizing church events, and, he enjoyed it, especially as the church was a mere two minute walk from his home.

Sometimes though, Ignatius would be briefly transported back to his time serving his country, and his years in the army; May would sometimes catch him seemingly staring into space. He missed it, he even missed teaching, which he had loved equally, but it was no comparison to the camaraderie, excitement and the sheer adrenaline rush he had experienced in combat.

May had planned to retire at the age of 60. She wanted to travel, and though Ignatius had seen much of the world, his army career taking him overseas on numerous occasions, May had never left Georgia. He recalled how he would count the days to her retirement, so they could spend their remaining years growing old together, taking cruises, extended vacations, visiting distant relatives and traveling not just the globe, but their own country.

But plans don't always work out, life, as Ignatius well knew, was fragile, and even though it was a cliché, it was true, bad things did indeed happen to good people. May had been a good woman, and back then, he had considered himself a good man.

Ignatius' mouth was dry and he took another sip of water from the glass by the side of his bed. Soon his suffering would be over and he hoped that wherever he was headed, May would be waiting for him.

Ignatius Jackson had been a brave and honorable man, a man May was proud to call her husband, and seventeen years ago he would have shuddered at the very thought of being involved in a business that solicited death and murder. But things change, people change, perspectives change and the human condition can be driven by many things, and, despite his former honor, integrity and righteous beliefs, Ignatius had been driven by anger and revenge. How different things would have been if it hadn't been for the fact that his precious May, the one true love of his life, who had sacrificed her dreams to be a mother, due to the chemicals he had infected her with, who had cared for him and helped him not beat, but at least fend off cancer had, for all intents and purposes, been murdered, and the man who killed her left unpunished….

# CHAPTER FOUR

It had been a normal Tuesday, that fateful day seventeen years ago. May had left Gordonston and driven to the hospital where she was now a Senior Sister, in charge of the emergency room nursing staff. Ignatius had been as good as his word; he had taught his wife how to drive and, as he had promised, bought her a car. Many times he had offered to replace it, to buy her a new one, but she had refused. She had driven the same car for twenty years, she was comfortable with it, it was safe, and anyway, who needed a new fancy car? There was nothing wrong with it.

Ignatius had spent the morning following his usual routine. He walked to the church, and had spent the morning organizing a trip for some of the children, who attended the Sunday school, to visit the zoo in Atlanta. That afternoon he trimmed the flowers, read the newspapers, took a stroll in the park and prepared an evening meal for May's return home that evening. Everything that day was fine, the weather glorious, his health fine, and it was a day closer to May's retirement. He had kissed his wife, as he had every morning for the past 35 years, as soon as he awoke, which was always at six. He had told her that he loved her, that he cherished her, and that he was proud of her, again, as he did every morning. In turn, she had told him to "stop being such a softy," something she said every morning.

May Jackson was tired. It had been a long and arduous day. It seemed most days were now seemingly becoming longer. It was her age, she often thought; she wasn't as young, or as sprightly as she had once been. She also seemed to, just lately at least, spend more time doing paperwork than actual nursing. Writing never-ending reports, evaluating the younger nurses and dispensing advice and guidance not only to her designated nursing staff but to junior doctors, senior doctors, consultants and on the odd occasion, to the women who worked in the canteen. She was well respected, and the staff, not just the medical staff, but all at Memorial Hospital would miss her when she retired in less than three weeks.

At 2.30 pm, her sister called. May's sister, Emma, lived on Tybee Island, ten miles east of Savannah and a short drive from May's home in Gordonston. Emma was also a nurse, and five years younger than her sister. On occasion, May would, after work, visit her sister for sweet tea and to catch up on the family gossip, before returning home to spend the remainder of the evening with her husband.

May confirmed that she would be stopping by to see her sister once her shift had ended, not to partake in chit chat and sweet tea, but because her sister was sick. She had asked May to collect a prescription for her, as she felt too unwell to leave the house. Unlike May, her sister had not met the man of her dreams, and was a childless spinster.

It was around 4.30 pm that the first casualty arrived at the emergency room. A fire had broken out at a hotel in downtown Savannah. Hundreds were injured, suffering from injuries that ranged from smoke inhalation to serious burns. The emergency room was swamped, patients were being treated in the waiting area, and triages had even been set up in the car park. May had not hesitated to volunteer and stay late to help with the emergency, despite her shift officially ending at four. She had called Ignatius and told him that she would be home late, that she had no idea when she would be returning, that she also had to collect her sister's prescription. May told Ignatius not to wait up, it could even be an 'all-nighter'. She told him to eat, and she explained to him that she was needed, that it was all hands on deck. Of course he had understood. That was May, selfless, caring and professional – he wouldn't have expected anything less.

The emergency room teams had worked through the night, and thanks to their dedication and, not least of all, the leadership shown by Senior Sister May Jackson, not one casualty succumbed to their injuries. She was hailed by many that night as a hero. Yes, she was exhausted, and yes, the night had now turned into early morning, but lives had been saved, the injured cared for and families grateful that the staff on duty that night had, as one survivor later said, performed miracles.

May Jackson was a safe, experienced and good driver. She had of course been taught to drive by Ignatius, and in her twenty years of driving had never once so much as gotten a scratch on her car, received a speeding ticket, nor even a parking ticket. Normally she did not drive in the dark and, as her position meant she no longer worked late shifts, or other unsociable hours, she rarely drove at night. That evening, now early morning, had been the exception. Of course she was tired and even exhausted. It had been a long and traumatic day; however, she was certainly safe to drive. There was no question of that. If she hadn't been, she would have called Ignatius, who would have driven to the hospital to collect her.

Her home was less than five miles away from the hospital, a short distance that she had driven many times before, but of course she had an important errand to run. She had not forgotten about her sister, and her promise to collect her prescription. Despite Emma's protestations, May would still drive to the pharmacy, pick up her sister's medication, deliver it and then return home. It would only take her a few minutes, and anyway, she had explained, the roads would be clear, and a promise is a promise.

May drove the fifteen miles to Tybee Island, luckily her sister's prescription was being administered by a pharmacy that was open twenty four hours a day. She collected it on behalf of Emma, duly delivered it to her sister, spent ten minutes describing the events that occurred that day at the hospital, declined a glass of sweet tea and then began her journey home.

As she had expected, the road leading from Tybee Island to Savannah was clear of traffic, her headlights were on, her seat belt fastened, and her speed did not exceed any limit that had been imposed on US 80, the stretch of road that connected Tybee to Savannah.

Thomas Robertson, known as TJ to his friends and family, had been drinking all night. He was drunk. After consuming several bottles of beer, numerous shots of whiskey and a bottle of wine he was in no fit state to walk, let alone drive. But TJ Robertson didn't care. Why should he? He was rich, his father was rich, and he could do what he wanted. Even if a cop did pull him over, so what? His father would pay them off; he always did. Despite being an habitual drunk driver, TJ Robertson had not once gotten a ticket, despite being pulled over on numerous occasions, as he headed home, as he did every night, from his bar hopping in Savannah, along US 80, back to his Tybee Island beach house.

In an ideal world their paths would not have crossed. In an ideal world, TJ Robertson would not have been drunk, he would have simply passed May's car as she passed his. In an ideal world, TJ Robertson would have been traveling on the right side of the road.

May had stood no chance. It could only be speculated what went through her mind as she saw the headlights approaching her at top speed. She had braked, tried to swerve out of the way, but it had been too late. The collision flipped her car and it rolled several times before landing in the marsh that saddled both sides of US 80. TJ Robertson's car also flipped over and careened into a tree. Ten minutes later, a motorist in a car heading from Tybee to Savannah pulled over after spotting the wreckage and called the emergency services.

Less than one hour after leaving the emergency room, where she had battled to save so many lives, May Jackson returned; this time fighting for her own life. At 4:45 am she succumbed to her injuries and died on the operating table. TJ Robertson survived. Though unconscious when brought into the hospital, his only injuries were a few scratches and a broken wrist. Later he would call it a miracle, divine intervention from God, which had spared his life.

# CHAPTER FIVE

"Who the heck is that?' muttered Ignatius as he made his way to the front door of his home, dressed in his dressing gown and wearing his slippers. "Is that you, May?" he shouted. "Did you forget your door key? So much for just going to sleep. It's five in the morning! I will be getting up soon," he continued jokingly, as he opened the door to his home. Ignatius was not at all surprised his wife was this late. She had of course forewarned him that she would be working late. It must have been a busy night, and then no doubt she had spent a few hours gossiping with her sister. She was probably too tired to even find her door key, which he guessed was stuffed deep inside her purse.

The doorbell rang again. "Hold on, I am coming. Hold your horses, May, I am not opening this door naked," he shouted once again as he opened the door.

"Ignatius Jackson? Mr. Ignatius Jackson?" asked the young looking police officer at his door.

"Yes, son, that's me," replied Ignatius. "Hey, don't I know you?" he said, a look of recognition engulfing his face. "Didn't

I teach you at Savannah High?"

The young officer nodded. "Yes, sir, you did, John Fuller."

"John Fuller," repeated Ignatius. "I remember you. Damn fine footballer if I recall. Well, look at you, son, all grown up and a police officer. I always knew you would do well. Now tell me, son, why are you banging on my door and ringing my bell at five o'clock in the morning? You are lucky my wife isn't here. After she had scolded you, she would have you eating cookies and milk and have you telling her your life story."

Officer John Fuller took a deep breath. "Mr. Jackson, that's why I am here. It's your wife; she has been involved in an accident."

Ignatius smiled. "I know that, son. That's where she is now, dealing with the accident, the fire at the hotel. I know all about it. Don't worry, I know they probably sent you to let me know she ain't coming home yet. Come in, son, take a seat. I will fix you some coffee, and maybe you can take a sneaky five minute break."

"You need to come with me, please, sir, come with me." John Fuller loved his job, but this particular task of being a police officer was one he hated. It was especially hard, as he had nothing but affection for Ignatius Jackson. Everyone had; every kid who had ever met him, while he was teaching, had a soft spot for Ignatius. It had been the officer's decision to be the one to deliver the bad news to Ignatius. His partner, Sergeant Taylor, who sat waiting in the squad car parked in the street outside, had offered to do it, but John Fuller had insisted.

Ignatius arrived at Memorial hospital thirty minutes after his wife died. He did not get the chance to say goodbye, to tell her how much he loved her, how sorry he was that she had never been a mother, how proud he was of her. Her friends and colleagues at the hospital had tried desperately to save her. Though she was dead, they had tried to revive her non-beating heart. No one had wanted to make the call, no one wanted to give up on her, but it was pointless, even if she had recovered, regained consciousness and a heartbeat, her skull and torso had been crushed, and her brain had ceased functioning the moment TJ Robertson had hit her car.

Officer Fuller, accompanied by Sergeant Taylor, explained to Ignatius what had happened, explained the head-on collision, and explained that May was not responsible, explained that they believed the other driver, who was still unconscious, had been drinking, and that he had crossed into her lane. Paramedics had stated that the other driver had reeked of alcohol, and they had concluded that he must have been drunk. When, and if, he regained consciousness, a blood sample would be taken, and a breath test administered, and of course charges would be filed.

The officers were joined by the attending doctor, his scrubs covered in May's blood. He explained to Ignatius, that his wife had not suffered, that she had arrived at the hospital unconscious, and that it was highly unlikely that she had suffered any pain. The words flew over Ignatius as he stood in disbelief. He steadied himself and was aided by Officer Fuller and Sergeant Taylor and led to a chair. He was used to death, used to tragedy, but this was different. In a flash his whole life had crumbled. May, his beautiful May, his lover, friend, companion and soul mate, gone. Their future, gone. Their happiness, gone. In an instant.

"Can I see her?" he asked, his composure slowly returning.

The doctor shook his head. "I am not sure that is wise. You may want to remember how she was. Her injuries were quite traumatic." Ignatius stared into space. He noticed young nurses weeping, he could also see that the physician before him was trembling, and the redness around his eyes indicated that he to, had shed a tear for May Jackson.

"Son, I spent 8 years in Vietnam, I cradled dying boys with no limbs, with half their heads blown off. I think I can handle saying goodbye to my wife."

The doctor nodded; he understood. He knew, from May,

about Ignatius, his medals, his valor, his war time service. Normally he would have refused such a request, but not this time. The doctor led Ignatius through the emergency room waiting area and into the operating theater, where his wife's body lay. Ignatius took her hand and held it tightly. It was true; she was unrecognizable, but that did not deter or waiver Ignatius' resolve. He turned to the doctor.

"Every morning, son, for the last 40 years, I have kissed this woman. This morning will be no exception." Ignatius bent over his wife's lifeless body and kissed her forehead.

The days and weeks following May's death were the hardest of Ignatius's life. Numerous tours of Vietnam, postings in some of the most dangerous places in the world, were nothing compared to the anguish he felt. He had never felt so alone. The house was filled with May's possessions, the echo of her perfume lingered in the air. He was a mess, and he felt he had lost his will to live. He sometimes expected his wife to walk through the door, and that surely this was all a nightmare. It should have been him who was buried at Bonaventure Cemetery, not May. He should be the one who was dead.

Ignatius had no idea how he could face life without May. He didn't know how long he had anyway, and without May, he was sure his life would have no purpose; he had simply nothing to live for. The only thing that kept him sane and indeed alive, for many were the times he contemplated taking his own life, was the fact he wanted to see justice done, and the man who had murdered his wife, for that is how Ignatius saw it, would never be able to hurt another soul again. TJ Robertson needed to pay for his crimes. Son of a rich man, privileged spoiled brat, it didn't matter. Ignatius wanted justice, and by God May deserved it.

Ignatius, though his faith in God was waning, still had faith in justice, had faith in the law, faith in the American way, faith in the 'system', the system he had served faithfully his whole life, as a soldier and as an educator.

But there was no justice.

TJ Robertson never did take a sobriety test. Nor was his blood ever tested for alcohol. Before anyone could even speak to him, after he recovered consciousness, they had to navigate past several of his father's high priced attorneys. The paramedics who had initially claimed that they had smelled alcohol on his breath recanted their statements. Pressured by attorneys who had argued that the smell of alcohol could have emitted from anywhere; maybe one of the empty bottles found in TJ Robertson's car had been the cause of the odor? There was no proof at all he had been drinking. As for the two attending police officers, they hadn't even spoken to poor TJ. It was conjecture and rumor, and there was no evidence. Yes, a few witnesses said they had seen him drinking earlier that evening, but was he drunk? Prove it.

There was now also a new spin on the cause of the accident. Hadn't May Jackson been working for over fifteen hours; wasn't she exhausted? She hardly ever drove at night. She was old; maybe, just maybe, it was she who had caused the accident. The attorneys were good, the best money could buy, and it didn't even go to trial.

In the months that followed, Ignatius hounded the DA to press charges, begged the police to investigate TJ Robertson. Surely he had a record? Surely there must be something, something they could do? How dare they pin this on May? How dare they shift her from victim to cause of the accident? Though they listened, the police could do nothing. Though Ignatius understood that the DA's hands were tied, that didn't help him. As time passed, Ignatius lost faith in the 'system' he had served. He lost faith in justice, and he lost faith in just about everything. He had lost faith in the law. His medals and ribbons, his service, meant nothing to him now, and it seemed to no one else.

As Ignatius's life spiralled downwards, alone and bitter, frustrated that no one would help him seek justice for May — and maybe even save the life of someone else who could become a victim of the drinking and driving habits of TJ Robertson – his life shattered. It had been a chance meeting with an old friend and comrade that had changed and redirected his life.

Lieutenant General Peter Ferguson, retired, had served under Major Ignatius Jackson during The Battle of Fire Support Base Ripcord, as a young 2nd Lieutenant. The 23 day battle between the U.S. Army 101st Airborne Division and **the** North Vietnamese Army, that occurred from July 1, 1970 until July 23, 1970, was the last major confrontation of the Vietnam War between United States ground forces and North Vietnam. Three Medals of Honor and six Distinguished Service Crosses were awarded to participants for actions during the operations. One of them to Ignatius Jackson, for saving the life, while under heavy fire, of his second in command, Peter Ferguson.

Peter Ferguson would be visiting Savannah, on private business, and had looked up the number of his old comrade and friend. It would be marvellous to see Ignatius and May again. Though they had lost touch over the years, he owed the man his life. Though it would only be a fleeting visit, maybe they could grab dinner before he flew back to Washington.

Ignatius had been surprised to hear from his old friend. He had of course followed his career, and was not the least surprised that he had achieved the rank of Lieutenant General. They had exchanged Christmas cards for a few years, but then, suddenly, Peter Ferguson, after retiring from the army, disappeared. Ignatius had lost contact with him, even his Christmas cards returned unopened. So it was an immense surprise when Ferguson called.

Ignatius explained to his friend, during that initial phone call, that May had passed away. He didn't go into details, but he would do, once they met, he would love to go to dinner with his former subordinate. Pete Ferguson had expressed his condolences for Ignatius's loss. May had been a good woman, and had been well liked and respected by all Ignatius's men.

Peter Ferguson had a proposal for Ignatius. He had something he wanted to discuss, face to face, something he couldn't talk about over the phone.

But Peter Ferguson had known that May was dead. He knew most things, and his call had not been by chance, but Ignatius didn't need to know that, not yet anyway....

# CHAPTER SIX

Kelly Hudd knew she needed to shower, but she didn't care. She hadn't showered in days. As she stared into the mirror, she could hardly recognize herself. Her once model like figure had gone. In the past few months she had piled on weight, fifteen pounds, give or take a few pounds. Her once perfect skin was blotchy and dry. Her hair was lank and unkempt, and her roots were now showing. Her fingernails had been chewed and gnawed, and she could not remember the last time she had indulged herself with a manicure. The woman staring back at her was a stranger to her, who bore no resemblance to the once beautiful, contented and happy woman she had once been.

She sighed heavily as she dressed in a bathrobe and headed from her bedroom, down the stairs to her sanctuary… the kitchen and her parent's fridge.

Kelly had been staying with her parents since Tom had left her. She had no desire to return to her old home or neighborhood. Atlanta was a good distance from Savannah and the memories of Tom. She did not care what became of her old home on Henry Street. It did not matter to her if it was falling apart, if the place was filthy; she didn't even care if it was even swallowed up by a sinkhole. It could burn, for all she cared. She paid no concern to the probable state of her lawn; she did not give a hoot if her once immaculate garden was now overgrown with weeds. Her life, as it had been, was over.

She had lost her job at Macy's, fired, after failing to turn up for work on six consecutive occasions. She hadn't called them anyway, her boss, nor her former colleagues, nor had she responded to the numerous phone calls from her worried supervisor, and she had simply ignored the letter that had arrived, informing her she had been terminated.

She was sure the house was probably in foreclosure anyway. She certainly could not afford the mortgage payments, nor the taxes due, even if she was working. They, she and Tom, had relied on both their salaries to keep the house, and to indulge in their penchant for fine clothes and expensive luxuries… not that that mattered, nothing mattered anymore.

Kelly opened her parent's refrigerator and inspected its contents. Shaking her head, not craving the block of cheese, nor the day old fried chicken, she closed the fridge door and opened the freezer compartment door and retrieved a carton of chocolate ice cream. This was her life now; this is how she coped; lying in bed, or sitting at her parent's kitchen table, probably now addicted to Xanax and gorging on ice cream. Broken hearted, depressed and with nothing to look forward to, for all intents and purposes, her life was over.

Her parents, though, had been fantastic: they had told to stay for as long as she wanted. Not to worry about a thing. She was their daughter after all, their only child, and of course Shmitty, who lay on the kitchen floor watching his forlorn mistress shovel spoonful's of ice-cream into her mouth, was welcome to live with them also.

Her parents had not asked too many questions. Kelly had

simply told them that Tom had left her. She did not explain why, she wasn't one hundred percent sure herself. They had respected her privacy, had tried to reassure her, that everything would be fine, that Tom would be back, that all marriages, sooner or later, had their downs, as well as their ups.

As she delved into the ice cream, Kelly felt empty and hollow inside. A continual pain in her stomach, a result of the clinical depression, for which she was now receiving therapy and treatment. She knew she had brought this all on herself. If only she hadn't gone to Paris, if only she had never met the ridiculous, deceitful, and conniving Billy Malphrus, if only Tom hadn't found out and left her.

Initially she had thought Tom might have been in trouble, maybe he had even been abducted. She remembered the morning he left her as if it were yesterday. She had been feigning sickness, trying to avoid the rat of a man living next door, with whom she had unwittingly had a one night stand; after he had lied to her and tricked her. Tom had taken Shmitty for his morning walk; it was usually her job to do that, but he still had a day of leave remaining, and of course, she was 'sick', and unable to even leave the house. An hour passed and Tom had not returned. Usually Shmitty would just run into the park, sniff around and run back to the gate, unless there were other dogs in the park. Then he would play; especially if The Gordonston Ladies Dog Walking Club were present with their canines.

She had peered from behind her curtains, too afraid to venture outside, should she encounter either Cindy or Billy, trying to spot Tom walking back with Shmitty. It had been Shmitty's crying that had forced her to open her front door. She had found Shmitty, his leash around his neck, sitting on his haunches, looking just as confused as she.

In a panic, she had dressed quickly and then driven the neighborhood looking for her husband. Her first stop had been the park; she had shouted his name from behind the gated entrance, before entering. She had continued to shout his name as she traversed every inch of the place, but he was nowhere to be seen. There was not even a hint, or trace that he had ever even been there.

She had then frantically knocked on Elliott Miller's front door. Since he lived opposite the park maybe he had seen Tom, or maybe heard something. Elliott had been kind, he had swapped his house slippers for shoes and insisted they go back to the park and search some more. He had a key to the scout hut; maybe Tom was in there? Elliott's and Kelly's combined search of the park proved to be fruitless; Tom was definitely not there. Next, the pair had driven through the neighborhood, crisscrossing every avenue and street, in their separate cars; still there was no sign of Tom. Elliott had asked Kelly to call her husband again on his cell phone, but it went straight to voicemail. Elliott had tried from his phone; again it had gone straight to voicemail.

Distraught and emotional, Kelly had burst into tears. Elliott had held her as she cried, "Where is he? Where is he?" But of course Elliott had no answer for her.

"This is all my fault. I knew it. I knew he would find out. I knew it. He has gone, Elliott. He has left me. I just know it," she had said through her tears to her neighbor.

"That's just silly," Elliott had reassured her, confused by her comments.

"He has. I did something terrible, and I know he has found out," sobbed Kelly, hugging Elliott, tears staining his immaculate white shirt.

Elliott had hugged her harder. "Look, let's call the police, they will sort this out, I am sure."

"You think so? You think they will help me find him? Oh, Elliott, what I have done?"

It was Elliott who called the police, who had responded to his call within minutes, well aware that the man placing the call could soon be their Mayor. Elliott had stayed with Kelly as she explained that her husband had just vanished, and that she and Elliott had searched everywhere. He had been there when they took her statement, and he had remained at her side as the police also drove through the neighborhood, carried out a cursory search of the park and returned without finding Tom.

The attending officers advised Kelly to wait a few days, then if Tom didn't show up, to report him as a missing person. They tried to reassure her that he would return soon, that maybe he had just gone to the store; that maybe there was a logical explanation for his mysterious disappearance.

"You don't understand," she had said, even more tears streaming down her pretty face. "I did something bad. I cheated on him. I don't know how he found out, but he did. What am I going to do?"

Neither the police nor Elliott had any answers. Elliott thanked the officers for their search and told them he would make sure Kelly followed their instructions, that if Tom hadn't resurfaced in a few days, that she would report him as a missing person. Elliott had then made sure Kelly made it safely home, following her in his car, as she drove the short distance back to there.

Kelly waited patiently for Tom to call, but he didn't. She called his parents, the fire department, spoke to his Captain, but they had not seen or heard from Tom since he had begun his extended leave period. After three days, Kelly reported Tom as a missing person.

She had asked Elliott to accompany her to the police station; she felt with him there they might take her seriously. Maybe with the Mayor-in-waiting at her side, they would be prompted to work especially hard to find her Tom.

Kelly and Elliott had been led through the station and had met with a detective, a man, Kelly thought who looked like a pig wearing glasses. Not a pig as in a derogatory term for a policeman, but he actually did resemble a pig. He asked a few questions, he enquired if Tom's car had been driven, but Kelly had told him no, it still sat in their driveway. In fact Tom's car keys still hung on the key rack in their hallway.

The piggy looking detective, who also smelled of offensive body odor, had sucked on his pen and leaned back in his chair, making notes where appropriate, while continually straining to read what he had written. Every now and then he would touch his thick glasses, adjusting them on his piggy round face. Kelly was surprised that this man was even a detective. Elliott, she had thought, also seemed rather shocked that this chubby, pig faced man, with his bald head and thick glasses, was a police officer. He certainly did not look like any detective she had seen on TV, or in the movies.

The detective promised to make some enquires. He would speak with some of her neighbors, try and find out if anyone had seen him the morning he disappeared. Later Kelly learned that Tom had spoken to a few of her neighbors. Several of them reported seeing him that morning heading to the park with Shmitty. They had all said the same thing; not one of them had seen anything suspicious, nor heard a sound, nothing untoward apparently had occurred. Tom had spoken with a few people, before he entered the park, but the park had been empty. Tom's disappearance appeared to be a complete mystery. Unexplained.

While making her initial missing persons report that day, with Elliott at her side, the chubby and odd looking detective had asked her if she had any thoughts on why Tom might have suddenly disappeared.

As he compiled his notes, the detective had looked up at Kelly, then glanced at Elliott, before speaking.

"So, there were no problems at home? I mean, he wasn't, as far as you are aware, seeing someone else? Maybe, and I hate to ask this, he had another woman?"

"No," Kelly said, her voiced raised, "Tom was, is, perfect, he would never cheat. No, that is simply not possible."

"Ok," said the detective. "Is there anything else I should know about?"

Kelly took a deep breath, and looked at Elliott, before

staring at her feet.

"Mrs. Hudd?" said the detective, "is there anything you would like to tell me?"

Kelly spoke sheepishly and in a whisper, conscious that her neighbor, Elliott sat with her. She felt embarrassed, she felt ashamed, but if what she told the police would help find Tom, then it didn't matter.

"Well, he may have found out that I had cheated on him," Kelly replied.

Elliott looked surprised, thought Kelly, though he did not comment. The detective began scribbling on his notebook.

"I see," he said, rather a little too judgmentally for Kelly's liking.

"But it wasn't anything serious," stammered Kelly. "To be honest I am not even sure he knew. It only happened last week. I was in France. It's a long story, but there was no way he could have found out." But Kelly wasn't sure. Maybe he had found out; maybe that's why he had left.

"Was it anyone he knew?" asked the detective, quickly glancing at Elliott before turning back to face Kelly.

"What are you suggesting?" interrupted Elliott, annoyed by the veiled implication. "I am her friend, her neighbor, her Alderman, probably soon to be the Mayor. If you are insinuating anything inappropriate between myself and Mrs. Hudd, I assure you, I will speak directly with the Chief."

The detective's demeanor changed immediately. Gone was his cockiness and his earlier condescending attitude.

"I apologize. I assure you I am not insinuating anything. Mr. Miller, Alderman, sir, please accept my sincerest apologies," he spluttered.

"I think you also owe Mrs. Hudd an apology, don't you?" said Elliott sternly.

"Yes, of course, I am sorry, for maybe subconsciously implying that the other man involved in your, erm, life, was Mr. Miller. I see he is here merely offering support, merely as a neighbor and friend, and of course, in his role as Alderman for your district, one of the finest I may say, Aldermen, not districts, though the district is also fine. I for one will be casting my vote next week in the mayoral election, and you, sir," he said turning back towards Elliott, "have my vote, sir." The detective shuffled uneasily in his chair, stains of perspiration appearing on his shirt under his armpits, the stench of his body odor increasing.

"Anyway, I digress, where was I? Oh yes, Mrs. Hudd, was your... dalliance with anyone Mr. Hudd may have known?"

"No," lied Kelly. "It happened in France. "He doesn't know him, the man I slept with," Kelly swallowed before adding, "and it was just once!"

Tom never did return to work, nor did he contact any friends or family. He must have been devastated, thought Kelly, finding out that she had been unfaithful, discovering that she had cheated on him. Facing Kelly after her treachery must have been too much for him, she guessed, and then having to see the man she had slept with, not that he was a man, he was a boy, a scrawny nasty little hick, well, that would have been worse. No, he was gone. He wouldn't have been able to take the ribbing from his friends, and he would have been the butt of countless jokes about how his beautiful wife had been tricked into sleeping with some horny kid pretending to be a count. The embarrassment would have been too much for Tom.

Of course Kelly hadn't given up searching immediately, she had continued to drive through every street and avenue in Savannah just hoping to catch a glimpse of her husband, but as the days and then weeks and eventually months passed, she resigned herself to accept the inevitable truth - Tom had left her and didn't want to be found. He had left her because somehow he had found out about Billy Malphrus, Paris and Count Enrico de Christo. Kelly knew she only had herself to blame.

The detective had called her a few times. He had no leads, and he had implied that many missing adults were missing because they wanted to be missing. They didn't want to be found. He had also told her that the department simply didn't have the resources or manpower to conduct a search on the scale Kelly had hoped, and of course, taking into consideration her confession of adultery, it was probably time for her to accept that Tom had simply left her.

Kelly took another scoop of ice cream as Shmitty continued to sleep at her feet. Tom had left everything, the only thing he had taken with him were the clothes on his back. She could remember exactly what he was wearing the day he had left her: lime green jogging pants and a white t-shirt. Those lime green sweatpants were a gift from her. She knew he hated them but he wore them nevertheless. Kelly began sobbing. How could it all have gone so wrong? How could she have destroyed her marriage, forced Tom to leave?

She turned her head to the refrigerator. The detective had given her his card. 'Detective Jeff Morgan' — and it now hung via a fridge magnet, along with other bits of paper, postcards and decorative fridge magnets collected by her parents.

At least Elliott had been good to his word. He had promised not to mention anything he had heard at the police station, Kelly's confession of adultery, nor any of the circumstances surrounding Tom's unexplained disappearance to a living soul. He hadn't, and she was thankful for that.

Maybe it was time for her to move on, to try and rebuild her life, despite her hopes that Tom would return. Maybe it was time to face facts. Maybe Tom was indeed gone for good and she would never hear from him again. Kelly Hudd had never not had a man in her life. She and Tom had been together since high school. Going forward, if she was to finally accept Tom was never going to return, she would, she was sure, need a man to support and love her. Kelly craved affection, and despite her current mental anguish and despair, she did not want to spend the rest of her life alone.

Kelly Hudd was shallow, and deep down she knew it. She was superficial and judged others by their looks, not their personalities. But she was evolving, she was changing, Tom's disappearance had given her time to take stock of her life and the way she lived it. At one time her looks had been the most important thing to her, and the second most important thing to her was how others looked. She was changing, and though consumed by many different emotions, including sadness, hate, insecurity and a lack of confidence, she remained practical. She knew she couldn't spend forever waiting for Tom, and she knew that sooner or later she would need to find a man to take care of her.

Shmitty stared at his mistress as she continued to shovel ice cream into her mouth. Shmitty, poor Shmitty, she thought. Tom had not only abandoned and left her, he had also left Shmitty. The poor animal had no idea what had happened to his master. He had no idea why they had left their former home and, thought Kelly, had no idea why he was no longer able to run in the park with his friends, the dogs belonging to The Gordonston Ladies Dog Walking Club.

# CHAPTER SEVEN

Ignatius had slept intermittently for a few hours. He looked down from his bed and saw that Chalky was still at his side. His dreams had been fuelled by his memories, and he had dreamt of May, Pete Ferguson and Chalky. A result, no doubt, of his reminiscing and the potent painkilling drugs he was taking to ease the horrendous pain caused by the cancer eating away inside him. He reached for one before lying back onto his bed, his eyes staring at the ceiling, and his memories once again fresh. He closed his eyes; it had been seventeen years ago.

* * * * *

Peter Ferguson and Ignatius had arranged to meet at Pete's hotel, a quaint Bed and Breakfast, named the Dresser Palmer House, located on Gaston Street, in downtown Savannah. Ignatius had walked the three miles from his home in Gordonston to the inn, which sat close to Forsyth Park and amongst the other fine homes which populated Savannah's downtown and tourist districts.

The walk would do him good. Though he was suffering a

broken heart, and had all but lost his will to live after May's death, he was still fit enough to briskly stroll to meet his old friend. Ignatius arrived promptly at the hotel. Despite his prolonged grieving and depressed mental state, he was excited at the prospect of seeing his old friend. Peter was waiting for him in the sitting room of the elegant inn.

"Ignatius," said Ferguson with a smile, as he gently grabbed his old friend and hugged him, "how long has it been? Twenty years? More? You look exactly the same," continued Ignatius's friend.

Ignatius Jackson smiled and shook his head. Young Pete Ferguson, a Lieutenant General, look at him, a little greyer than when he had last seen, a little fatter too, but here he was, dressed in an expensive looking business suit. For the first time in weeks, Ignatius smiled, and for a brief moment his depression, anguish and heartbreak evaporated as he embraced his old comrade.

"First of all, let me tell you how sorry and devastated I was when I heard about May. It was a shock, and please, accept my heartfelt condolences. She was a good woman, a great woman, and you have my utmost sympathies. I can only imagine the pain and suffering you are feeling."

Ignatius smiled. He knew his friend's words were genuine, and he had appreciated them.

"I am doing as well as can be expected I guess," he lied. "Thank you, Pete, for the kind words, May would have appreciated them. She was always fond of you."

"I am just sorry I wasn't here sooner. Sorry I didn't come for the funeral. I didn't know. I didn't find out until, well, you know, until I called," explained Pete.

Ignatius nodded and forced a smile. He understood. How would any of his old friends and comrades have known about his wife's death? It wasn't exactly news. There had been an obituary in the Savannah Morning News, but that had been it.

"Thank you, Pete, or should I call you sir?" joked Ignatius, referring to his former subordinate's high military rank which he had attained before his retirement from the military.

Peter laughed, before replying, "You know, it was me who always called you sir, when we served — the best commanding officer I ever had."

The retired General suggested they sit in the elegantly furnished and decorated sitting room, adorned with paintings and expensive furniture. "Nice place," commented Ignatius as he sat. The room, apart from the two men, was empty; in fact, the whole inn was deserted. All other guests were either sightseeing or conducting organized tours of the Hostess City. The innkeeper was away on errands. They were quite alone.

Ignatius enquired about Peter's family. His friend's wife and May had been good friends, and when they had known each other; often the two couples would dine together. His friend told him he and his wife had divorced several years ago, but he was sure that she was fine, especially after the alimony settlement she had received. For about an hour the two men recounted stories of their past, both mentioning names and characters that the other had long forgotten. Ignatius, for the first time since May's death, actually felt happy.

"Look, Ignatius," said Ferguson as he leaned in closer to his friend, checking over his shoulder that no one was in earshot. As the inn was deserted, he needn't have checked, but he did so anyway, his caution not going unnoticed by Ignatius.

"I am going to be honest. My being here, in Savannah, isn't a coincidence. I came here to see you and to speak to you. There is no 'other' business. I came because I have something I want to discuss with you. Something that I hope you will take seriously and, I am hoping, not be offended by."

"Okay," said Ignatius, intrigued by his friend's statement, "I am all ears."

"As I explained, I now work in the private sector. I know I told you that it was a security-based position, which I suppose it is, but my job is much, much more than that. My employers have many divisions, many subsidiaries; they are 'facilitators'; they get things done, for a price. They take care of things. I will be honest, I am not even sure who I work for, but I know we have contracts, contracts from the government, but, as I have been told a thousand times, I am just a small cog within a very big wheel."

Ignatius sat back in his chair and eyed his friend with curiosity. "Facilitators? What do you actually mean by facilitators? What is it you facilitate?"

Ferguson took a deep breath. "I work for a company known as the 'Organization'. They go by many different names; some are folklore, myth, even exaggerated, but I assure you that they are real. Some of our clients are wealthy individuals, and..." Ferguson once again looked around him, checking no one could overhear their conversation "...and even governments. We have sub contracted work for not only individuals but countries. This country, Ignatius, one of our clients is the CIA."

Ignatius shuffled in his seat and looked skyward before returning his gaze towards his friend. He had heard of 'organizations' before. They carried out 'Black Ops', 'Deniable Incursions' and 'Unauthorized Operations'. It was common knowledge, to Ignatius anyway, that there were 'organizations' who worked 'off the record' and 'under the radar', on behalf of governments.

"I am what is known as 'The Director'. I am the one responsible for fitting our guys for a certain job," explained Ferguson.

"Job?" interrupted Ignatius. "What type of job?"

"Job, as in contract, as in," once again Peter Ferguson looked around him, confirming that the two old friends were alone, "as in hits".

Ignatius whistled, amazed at what he was hearing. He sat back in his chair and smiled. So that was how Pete Ferguson afforded his flashy suit, the alimony he paid his wife, his flashy cars, his apartment in Manhattan, his town house in DC and his beach house in Miami.

"Oh, come on, Ignatius, don't act so surprised. You must realize that 'off the grid' things happen. They happened back when we were serving, and they still happen today. You know what I am talking about. Look at history, look at the world; there is dirty work to do and somebody has to do it." Peter Ferguson leaned back in his chair. "And I guess that someone is me."

Ignatius stared at his old friend. "It isn't that I am surprised. I assure you I am not. I am just surprised at how you found yourself such a cushy job? I am just surprised because the Pete Ferguson I knew, back in the day, was a straight-up guy, a stickler for order. It isn't this 'Organization' that surprises me. It's the fact you are involved. Let me get this straight," continued Ignatius, "you basically organize hit men to kill people. That, basically, is your job. I am correct?"

Peter Ferguson nodded.

"And you have both private clients and 'other' clients, who may, or may not be, working for governments, who subcontract your 'Organization' to carry out assassinations on their behalf?"

Ferguson nodded again. "Correct; I guess that's about the sum of it."

Ignatius put his finger to this lip and tapped it slowly before speaking again. "Peter, are you asking me to hire your 'Organization' to kill the man who murdered my wife? Don't bullshit me, son, I know you knew May was dead before you called, and if you are working for this 'Organization' I am sure you have eyes and ears everywhere. You know all about TJ Robertson, May's accident and the bull crap stunt they pulled, don't you?"

Ferguson laughed and shook his head. "No, Ignatius, I am not trying to get you to hire us. I am not a salesman, give me some credit. I am offering you a job; to join the 'Organization'; to replace me as the Director. You would be ideal. I know you may need some time to think about this, and of course I know this has come as a surprise, but I will be honest, you are the only man I trust."

Ignatius studied his friend before replying. "So, you are retiring?"

"No," replied Ferguson, "I will be the one in charge, your boss, but that's as much as you will ever know. We will never be able to socialize together, be seen together and our communicating will be over secure telephone and internet connections. It's a big ask, I know, but I promise you, I swear on the memory of May, that no matter what, I will protect you. You will be immune from any investigation or prosecution, there would be no link back to you, and I would not ask you, Ignatius, unless I had covered all eventualities."

Ignatius sat quietly, he gave his friend no indication as to what he thinking.

"And as for you hiring us to kill Robertson, I wouldn't dream of suggesting such a thing. That would be on the house."

Ignatius took a deep breath — that's what he wanted to hear. That was what he was waiting for, but he was cautious not to appear too willing.

"Pete, I don't know what to say. I mean, this is illegal, I know that, but why me?"

"You fit our profile, Ignatius. You have no family, and I am sorry to be blunt, you have no one. You are on your own. You were a hell of a sniper, a hell of a marksman, a hell of a soldier and a hell of a leader. You know how our contractors think. I respect your judgment, '*They*' respect your judgment. Yes, there is a risk, but as I said, I will protect you, always. We do have a certain 'agreement' with some very influential people. Though they do frown upon our private business, they leave us to our own devices. I mean, and I will be honest, people get hurt, people die, and sometimes they are people who don't deserve to die. But it is a business, Ignatius, a very lucrative business, and, as I see it anyway, if someone wants someone dead badly enough, then they will have them killed anyway. We can't stop it. We just provide the service."

"You mentioned Robertson," said Ignatius.

Ferguson nodded. "Yes. If you agree to join us, then the 'Organization' have agreed to take care of him; send in one of our contractors and take him out. Kind of a signing on bonus, if you like."

Ignatius shook his head. "No."

"No?" replied Ferguson.

"No. If I agree to join this organization, then I have one stipulation. One stipulation only. That I be the one who gets to kill Robertson."

"Ignatius, you are 61. You would be the prime suspect. This is the very reason we exist. To create distance between victims and those who want them dead. I am sorry, but I just couldn't risk it, and it goes against all our protocols."

"Pete, from what you have told me, you guys sound like you can do anything. I am sure that you can bend the rules just this once. It is personal; it is something I alone have to do. If I am going to 'direct' others to kill, then surely I should have had experience in the field. You know, Pete, I always led from the front."

Peter Ferguson knew that. He would be dead if Ignatius had not been there by his side in Vietnam, been there to drag him to safety, taking fire, and risking his own life, to save his second in command. It was his turn now, his turn to repay the debt.

Ferguson nodded his head. "We do have ways to provide you with a firm alibi, should you become a suspect, which let's face it, you probably would be. And we can set it up so that there will be no witnesses. Jesus Christ, we have killed Presidents and Kings and gotten away with it. Let me make some calls when I get back to DC. If I can arrange it that you are the one who pulls the trigger, the one who kills Robertson, are you in?"

Ignatius leaned back in his chair. "Hell, Pete, if you let me be the one to kill TJ Robertson, I would work for free."

Ignatius did not hear from Pete Ferguson for another three weeks. After shaking hands, Pete explaining that he had a flight to catch, they had parted. It was the last time he ever saw his friend.

Something had changed in Ignatius; his spirits and mood had improved, while still grieving for May, he suddenly felt he had a purpose again. If Pete had been telling him the truth, then Ignatius would have a renewed reason to live; he would become a harbinger of death for those who deserved it. His role as 'Director' would allow him to pick and choose which 'non-official' contracts the organization would accept, he would then allocate a suitable man for the job. It was now Ignatius's turn to administer justice. Not once on the day he joined the organization did he consider the innocents who might die.

Three weeks later Ignatius received several packages. One was a mobile telephone, the note that accompanied it informed him it was a secure and direct line, and this would be the chosen means of communication with the Organization. The other parcels contained a computer, printer, expensive office furniture, and other items that would not have looked out of place in a fancy Manhattan office. The note accompanying these packages advised Ignatius to go for a long walk tomorrow at two pm. and to return at four. When he returned, the equipment sitting in the large boxes, and the furniture provided, would have been set up for him. It was apparently a precaution; the fewer members of the 'Organization' who saw Ignatius, the better.

Five days after Ignatius had taken his ordered walk, and returned to find the room that overlooked Gordonston Park, the room in the turret that he had once earmarked to become a child's nursery, had been converted to a high tech office, the secure phone eventually rang.

It was Peter Ferguson. The Organization had agreed to Ignatius's terms. He was in. In a few minutes his computer would be remotely activated, files transferred, and he would begin his work as 'The Director' for the Organization immediately. Ignatius had only one question for his friend: when did he get to kill TJ Robertson?

Peter Ferguson explained that things had already been set in place, and that for the past four weeks they had had TJ Robertson under constant and clandestine surveillance. They knew his routine, his every move, they even knew what he had eaten for lunch four days ago. They had taken extra precautions for this one.

"Ignatius, are you sure you really want to go through this?" asked Pete.

Ignatius did not hesitate with his reply. There was no pause, no indication that he had for one minute changed his mind. "Yes."

"Good," replied Ferguson. "The kid's a menace. The guys watching him have reported that he hasn't learned his lesson. He is still drinking, still driving drunk. If you weren't going to do it, I would do it myself. For May, and the countless others this moron is potentially going to kill."

Ignatius was told that tomorrow morning a car would collect him from his home. The driver would have a package for him. They, Ignatius and driver, would then drive the approximate two hundred miles to Atlanta, where TJ Robertson was staying with his mistress. Not only was TJ Robertson a murderer, he was an adulterer, spending extended periods of time with his younger lover, holed up in the love nest he had provided for them, leaving his long suffering wife wondering where her husband was.

TJ Robertson was 29 years old, and during his brief time on earth had caused more misery, heartache and misfortune than ten men could in a lifetime. Ignatius had no reservations about killing this despicable man. For the first time in months Ignatius slept soundly, and the following morning he woke with a smile on his face.

As promised, a car was parked outside Ignatius's house; it was a black sedan.

As Peter Ferguson had predicted, the driver of the car handed Ignatius a package as soon as he entered the vehicle. He opened the carefully sealed box. The Beretta M9, Semiautomatic, 9mm, M9, was a 9×19mm Parabellum pistol adopted by the United States Armed Forces in 1985. Ignatius had not fired one of these weapons before, they had come into service after he left the army. He held it up in front of his eyes to enable him to take a better look at it. There was a silencer already attached.

"Are you ready, sir?" asked his driver.

"As I ever will be," replied Ignatius.

"Very well," said the vehicle's driver, a young man Ignatius guessed to be about 30 years of age, dressed in a dark suit, and sporting a short haircut. He shifted the car into drive and headed west towards Atlanta.

Three hours later Ignatius exited the vehicle and made his way to the spot where his driver had instructed he stand. The neighborhood was an upscale community; large spacious modern type homes; all with immaculate gardens and expensive looking cars parked in the driveways. It was not too dissimilar than his neighborhood in Savannah, thought Ignatius, though of course the homes had been built well after the houses in Gordonston. It was, as predicted by his driver, quiet. The streets, apart from a few vehicles parked on the road, were deserted. Ignatius checked the time on his watch. If his driver was correct, then TJ Robertson would be walking along this very avenue in precisely one minute. Ignatius checked his weapon, he double checked that the safety catch was off, he checked that the silencer was fitted correctly, checks he had carried out during the journey, but checks he nevertheless carried out again.

TJ Robertson, it seemed, had a routine. According to the surveillance reports, he and his girlfriend would party late into the evening, they rarely woke before noon. At 12:30, every day, TJ Robertson would go for a walk, an excuse to smoke a cigarette and to walk the puppy he had bought his lover as a gift. He would walk the quiet neighborhood until the young dog had done his business and he had smoked his first cigarette. He followed the same route every day. Today would be no different.

As Ignatius spotted Robertson turn a corner and head towards where he lay in wait, he had no second thoughts, no regrets and no fear of taking this man's life. This was the man who had destroyed his own life, killed the only person who he had ever loved. Ignatius was a trained killer; he had seen combat, fought in wars. Killing wasn't an easy thing to do, but for Ignatius – this killing would be, he would enjoy it.

TJ Robertson, with his girlfriend's puppy following him a few steps behind him on a leash, lit a cigarette as he reached the spot where Ignatius lay in wait. Without a word Ignatius fired one shot into his head. He fell to the ground without a sound. No one heard or saw anything; it was over in less than a second. Ignatius stared at the brindle puppy, who had not made a sound. The dark furred dog stared back at him. Ignatius took aim.

Five seconds later the black sedan appeared, the rear door ajar. As Ignatius entered the car a black van appeared from the other direction. As Ignatius's car sped away he turned his head to see two men lift the dead body of TJ Robertson into the back of the van before it sped off in the opposite direction from where Ignatius and his driver were headed. It was done. May had been avenged, justice had been served, and Ignatius felt no guilt, or the slightest bit of remorse for the man he had just executed.

"Well done, sir," said his driver, who glanced at Ignatius through his rear view mirror. Ignatius did not respond. "It's good to see someone lead by example. It will be a pleasure to work with you," continued the driver.

Ignatius once again did not reply.

"One thing though, sir," said his driver again. "I am not sure it was wise bringing the dog. I won't say anything, but it seems you are taking an unnecessary risk. Why didn't you just shoot it?"

Ignatius smiled and stroked the animal on his lap. He could not bring himself to harm it, nor could he face leaving it behind. Again he did not reply.

"I believe it is a Cairn terrier, if I am not mistaken," said his driver. "He looks young, probably only a few weeks old. My aunt has one, very loyal apparently. You know the dog from the Wizard of Oz was a brindle Cairn terrier, just like him."

Ignatius petted the animal on his lap and looked at his collar. He had a name tag… 'Blacky'.

"Just take me home, son," said Ignatius, "just take me home."

* * * * *

Ignatius Jackson once again coughed, blood splattering his handkerchief. Chalky again raised his head and whimpered softly. Ignatius reached over to his bedside table and grabbed a glass of water. He drank slowly before replacing the glass and laying his head back onto his pillow.

The body of TJ Robertson had never been found. Some had speculated that maybe he had been kidnapped, and that his father had refused to pay any ransom, others supposed that maybe his long suffering wife had been involved in his disappearance. One thing though was for sure, no one had even suspected Ignatius Jackson; he had not been questioned; there were no visits from detectives; nor was there any inclination that he could have possibly been involved. Peter Ferguson, though, had been annoyed and mildly disappointed with Ignatius for taking the dog. It was dangerous and stupid; the dog could have led the police back to Ignatius. But Ignatius had told his old friend, former subordinate and now boss not to worry. He had taken precautions, and did he really think he was going to leave an innocent puppy wandering the streets, let alone kill it, or leave it for the men who had retrieved Robertson's body, just for them to put a bullet in its head? No, it was fine, he had the dog, he had bleached and dyed his fur and changed his name. The puppy was his now, and his name was now Chalky.

Once again Ignatius returned from his memories as he coughed and noticed that now blood was dripping from his nose. He had resigned as the Director four months previously, a week after he had witnessed the killing of Tom Hudd by Doug Partridge. He had been thankful that Doug had not harmed Tom's dog, merely let him wander around the park, it was something Ignatius would have done.

The following day he had collapsed at home and the Doctor had given the prognosis – he had months to live, finally the cancer was winning, and the fact he had lasted as long as he had had been, according to his physician, remarkable. The Organization had accepted his resignation, he had spoken to Peter Ferguson personally, using a secure line, and though Ignatius half expected a visit from a 'contractor' to ensure his resignation was permanent, the waited bullet to his brain never came. What did come though was another message from Pete. The Organization had been compromised. It was over. There would be no more killings for the foreseeable future. A new Director had not been appointed to replace Ignatius, for the time being the 'Organization' would cease to exist. Who had compromised them wasn't known, what was known was that some names of 'contractors' had been leaked, and were now being auctioned to the highest bidders. Foreign governments, criminal organizations and even private individuals may have gotten hold of names and addresses of those who worked for the 'Organization'.

Ignatius Jackson did not know who had been compromised; he did not know whose identities and personal details had been on the stolen list. He didn't really care; the organization no longer existed. Soon he would no longer exist, so it didn't matter. But something compelled him to write the letter. It was against all protocol, against all the rules of the 'Organization', but he had written and sent it anyway. It wasn't for *him*, it wasn't to protect *him*, it was to protect the child....

# CHAPTER EIGHT

"At last!" cried Cindy Mopper as her doorbell finally rang. She had been waiting pensively for hours for her visitor and now he was here. She rushed to the front door and opened it with a smile on her face the length of the Savannah River.

"You're here! You're back!" she shouted as she opened the door to greet her visitor.

Billy Malphrus did what any dutiful and loving nephew would do. He hugged his aunt and kissed her on the cheek. Cindy beckoned him into the house, and along with his rucksack and battered suitcase, Billy entered the house he had left four months previously.

"Oh, Billy, it is so good to have you back," said Cindy as she handed her nephew a glass of sweet tea. "You have no idea what has happened here since you left. I don't know where to begin. Anyway, before I do, first tell me what you have been up to."

Billy smiled at his aunt, and took a sip of the sweet tea before he began his story.

He had spent the past few months in Africa, working for

yet another charity, this time helping to dig wells in remote villages. The charity had contacted him and practically begged him to go and help them out. They needed him, and what could Billy say? He couldn't refuse, even if it did mean leaving Savannah in the middle of night and having once again to leave his loving aunt. It had been hard and arduous work, and he had simply fallen in love with Africa and the villagers. They had practically pleaded with him to stay, even after the wells had been dug, and fresh water was now available to all. It was difficult to leave, but he had another priority, his beloved Aunt Cindy, and he simply had to return to Savannah and Gordonston to see her. He had called her the previous day from the airport, letting her know he was back and could he visit. Of course Cindy had replied yes. Visit? He could stay as long as he wanted. Who could turn away Billy?

The truth, though, was that Billy had never been to Africa. There was no village, and there were no wells to be dug. The morning Tom Hudd disappeared, Billy had noticed a police car parked outside the Hudd's home, next door to his aunt's house. Obviously he thought Kelly had turned him in. She had no doubt called the police and at that moment was making a statement about how she had been duped into sex by him, how he had pretended to be a 'Count', how he was nothing more than a conman who duped people out of money and unsuspecting women into sleeping with him. Was it a crime? Billy had no idea, but he wasn't going to hang around to find out. He had packed his bags and awakened his aunt who was still sleeping. He had told her he needed to go to Africa, and he had invented his story about wells, remote villages and how a charity had called him on the phone only a few minutes earlier. He would stay for lunch, then would have to leave that evening, he was just waiting on airline tickets, which would be e-mailed to him soon. Cindy had given him $50 for a taxi, and though she had tried to call Tom next door, to see if he would take her nephew to the airport, his phone had gone straight to his voice-mail greeting.

That evening, Billy had taken a cab, not to the airport, but to the bus station, and he had boarded a Greyhound to Florida. For the past four months he had been working as a busboy at a diner in Jacksonville, less than 200 miles from Savannah, a job from which he had been recently fired for stealing the tips left for the wait staff. He had called his aunt a few days before, not for the first time in his life virtually penniless and without a plan, and told her he was thinking of visiting her, once he returned from Africa. It had been his intention to simply ask for money, for the Africans of course, but when his aunt had mentioned that she was quite lonely, due in part to the fact her neighbor and friend Kelly had moved out of her house over three months ago to live with her parents, Billy's plan had changed. The coast was clear for him to return to Gordonston for an extended period, and there was now a second chance for him to maybe help himself to the loot and treasures he just knew would be stashed away in those old houses occupied by old biddies and Cindy's friends and neighbors.

"So she is gone then? The girl next door?" asked Billy innocuously as he took a bite of the third ham sandwich, which his aunt had dutifully made him, as he finished recounting his false stories of Africa.

"Yes, and it is all very sad. He just vanished, Tom. You remember him? He picked you up from the airport when you came back from India. Anyway, some people think he may have had another woman. But you know me, Billy, I am not one for gossiping or spreading rumors. Apparently he just got up one morning and like that," Cindy clicked her fingers, "he was gone. Not a trace of him. Probably living a double life. It was the same day you left, very strange. You know some people do, live double lives? You never can tell."

Billy nodded, not realizing the irony of his aunt's last statement.

"So what happened to her?" asked Billy, appearing concerned for the poor girl next door. "Kelly? Where is she?"

"Well, you never met her, did you? I remember now. She was sick, some virus or something. Such a shame. You would have liked her, very sweet girl."

Billy confirmed that he had never met Kelly, and expressed his disappointment that he hadn't.

"So, she moved in with her parents in Atlanta. She took Shmitty with her, that's her dog, and just left, about three weeks after Tom did. So sad. I think the house is being taken back by the bank, it must be, I am sure. Such a shame. She just left it how it was; left the furniture, all her clothes I am sure, everything. You should see her garden, Billy. It is overgrown with weeds, and the lawn really needs mowing. It is becoming a bit of an eyesore really, kind of bringing down the neighborhood, if you ask me. Poor girl. I heard that she had a nervous breakdown, but I don't know. Just gossip, something I don't ever listen to. It's all very sad." Cindy sighed.

"And it's a mystery," continued Cindy. "I mean, I just can't imagine Tom just leaving her like that. I would love to know who the other woman is; of course, that is not none of my business, and I wouldn't want to spread any rumors. But he was so handsome, so rugged, so fit, I would think he could have his pick of women," Cindy paused for breath before continuing, "but Kelly is beautiful. It is very strange; they were the perfect couple. But who really knows what goes on behind closed doors?"

Billy nodded, indicating to his aunt that he concurred with her statement. He remembered the last time he had seen Tom, heading towards the park. After Billy had returned from taking Paddy for a walk, and smoking a cigarette, he had spotted Tom walking along Atkinson Avenue, wearing those ridiculous and hideous lime green sweat pants. Billy shrugged, well, at least she was gone, the liar and the fraud, Kelly Hudd, and as an extra bonus, her house was empty, no doubt filled with items he could steal and probably sell. The Hudd's situation could prove very profitable for Billy, he thought, as he took another bite of his sandwich.

"Well, you relax, my dear, and if there is anything you need you just holler," said Cindy. "Nothing is too much trouble for my Billy," she continued, patting her nephew on the knee.

Cindy then proceeded to tell Billy all her other gossip and news, mostly focusing on her neighbours. Billy listened with feigned interest as his aunt gave him a blow by blow account of Elliott Miller's mayoral campaign and the highly likely chance he would win the election. Billy stifled a yawn when she told him Doug Partridge had probably left his wife, and he had to stop himself from falling asleep as Cindy talked about her friends Carla and Heidi. The only time Billy showed any interest in anything his aunt said was when she once again mentioned Kelly and Tom Hudd.

"Poor girl. Gone. Completely gone. Haven't seen her for months. And him, well, what on earth is he thinking? He must have found another woman. So sad. You never actually met her, did you, Billy?" said Cindy, repeating herself and revolving the conversation back to whence it had started.

Billy shook his head, becoming slightly irritated that Cindy was doing what she always did, repeating herself and reiterating conversations they had already had. "No, wouldn't recognize her if I bumped into her," he lied. "Such a shame though, it sounds, that people do that to each other. Why can't people just be nice to each other?" asked Billy.

Cindy hugged her nephew again. "Maybe if people were more like you," she said.

Billy Malphrus was tiring of his act, and he was tiring of Cindy. He didn't enjoy staying with her; it was a necessity. He wasn't interested in anything she said and he couldn't care less about Heidi, Elliott, Carla, Doug or any of her friends. If it wasn't for the money she gave him, and the fact she waited on him hand and foot, he wouldn't even come and visit. And, of course, the potential opportunity that existed for him to steal from her friends.

How could his aunt be so dumb? She had to be the easiest

person in the world to fool, apart from of course Kelly Hudd. She hung onto his every word, believed every word he said, sucked in his lies, and worshiped him. Billy was slowly coming to despise the woman, despite all she did for him. The fact she was the only person on the planet who so much as gave two hoots about him did not register with Billy. She was stupid, pathetic, but Billy envied her easy simple life. No money worries, she could do as she pleased. No sleeping rough for her, no working twelve hour days for minimum wage for Cindy. No. She had had it easy her whole life. She had married a rich man and inherited his money. Piddling around with her stupid friends and gushing over that Elliott Miller. She had a perfect little life, thought Billy, she had never worked a day in her whole life. It wasn't fair, she had pots of money, no responsibilities and spoiled her dog more than she did him.

Billy smiled at his aunt. "I love you, too" he said, as he returned her hug.

Paddy stared at Billy who was lying on the rug in the den. Billy didn't like Paddy much either. Spoiled rotten. The dog probably ate better than he did. He doubted that dog had a care in the world, waited on by his stupid aunt all day, all the dog seemed to do was eat and sleep. That was the life Billy wanted.

"Another sandwich, Billy?" asked Cindy.

Billy nodded. "Oh, yes please."

Paddy tilted his head to the left as he stared at Billy, hoping that he would throw him a piece of ham. *You can forget it,* thought Billy, *you aren't getting anything from me.*

# CHAPTER NINE

Pete Ferguson knew he was facing a tough task. The Organization was in tatters; they had been the victims of hacking. Despite their security levels and precautions, someone, somehow, had gotten hold of an electronic file listing the names of several of their contractors. To make matters worse, a Senator had started asking questions, questions about 'Black Ops', clandestine operations, and 'plausible deniability'. He wanted a house investigation to provide answers he was not getting from certain government agencies. There would, of course, have been an easy solution to the senator's snooping, but killing him, even if they made it look like an accident, would just bring more heat onto the already under pressure Organization.

The first task at hand for Peter Ferguson, though, was dealing with the leak. Those named on the stolen list were sitting ducks, their lives very probably in jeopardy, but worse for Ferguson and the Organization, they provided a lead and a link to them. It was every man, and woman, for themselves.

All operations had been canceled. The Organization had,

for all intents and purposes, disappeared. Computers and mainframes wiped, bank accounts closed; it would be virtually impossible for anyone even trying to even prove they existed, or had ever existed.

Peter Ferguson's only task was now to tie up loose ends. He could take no chances, he had no idea how large the leak was, and as he went through the list of names before him, marking those contractors and former employees who would soon be receiving a visit from an elite team of killers, handpicked men that Ferguson knew had not been compromised, with a red cross, he felt a tinge of guilt. Some of these men, and women, had been recruited by him, some had been former friends. Now, he was marking them for death, before they could talk, before they could be tortured for information. In a way, thought Ferguson, maybe he was doing them a favor. Maybe by marking them for death he was saving them from a far worse fate; governments and individuals hell bent on revenge, long prison terms and the stripping of assets. With his contractors dead, there could be no trials, if it ever came to that, and without trials and proof of any wrongdoing, their hidden bank accounts would be safe. In a way, he was assuring security for the families of his former killers.

He opened up the latest encrypted e-mail he had just received. It contained a list of outstanding contracts, and each contract named was linked to an electronic file, detailing the particulars of the 'job' requested, jobs that had been paid for, but not yet carried out. While perusing the files, one caught his eye almost immediately. It was simply titled "Gordonston".

He opened the electronic file and downloaded the contents to the secure hard drive of his laptop. Three outstanding contracts, all within the same neighborhood, ironically the same neighborhood as his friend and the now retired 'Director', Ignatius Jackson. He leaned forward at his desk and began reading, shaking his head in disbelief at the contents of the file. What a neighborhood, he thought, removing his glasses and rubbing his forehead. He began to type… just one word. Canceled.

As he sat at his desk, Ferguson found it hard to comprehend how many people so quickly resorted to murder to settle their differences. It wasn't just private individuals, such as the three women in Savannah, whose contracts he had just canceled, but countries and governments. How quickly the human race resorted to violence. He doubted any one of the victims who had just been reprieved from death deserved to die.

Another encrypted e-mail arrived in his inbox. He opened it immediately. The title of the e-mail read 'Jackson?' - There was no text or message. Peter Ferguson did not hesitate, he replied immediately:

"Jackson — NO Termination — leave him alone".

Pete Ferguson was well aware that the Organization was in trouble. Despite their work for various governments, and some partial immunity from scrutiny, the knives were out. He was unsure who exactly had compromised them, but the rumor was it had been a foreign government.

As head of the Organization he had had no choice. It was time to hide. To disappear. To erase all traces of the Organization, and to sever the connections of all those who had links to it. When he discovered that a computer file containing the identities of some of the Organization's associates had been compromised and was being offered for sale to the highest bidder, he knew that it was over.

His only concern was for his friend Ignatius Jackson; he must be protected at all costs. He owed him that. Ferguson had broken protocol and contacted Ignatius directly, informing him that it was time to 'clean up' loose ends. That every known contractor was now a target, not just a target of the Organization's enemies but the Organization itself. There could be no links back to those who controlled the Organization. The implications of the world discovering that governments used hired guns to carry out their dirty work was bad enough, but to learn that these hired guns also killed anyone for money were unthinkable. Senate hearings and possible impeachments were one thing, but the global consequences could be disastrous.

Ignatius had sounded sick, throughout their brief telephone call he had coughed continuously and his voice had sounded weak. No matter what, Ignatius Jackson would remain protected. Ignatius had surprised Pete with one request – a request that initially he had steadfastly refused, but Ignatius had been adamant. He wanted just one thing, one final favor.

Peter Ferguson eventually agreed. It was the least he could do for his oldest and best friend.

# CHAPTER TEN

He had just one more suitcase to unpack. He had arrived with three, just clothes, toiletries and a few mementos to decorate his new temporary home. The flight to Savannah had been quite uneventful. He had, of course, flown first class from his departure point, and though the flight had been long, over eight hours, he had enjoyed it. Thankfully, none of his old family photographs had been damaged during the flight, and his luggage, though having traveled on three separate flights, had arrived, as he had, intact and on time.

The house he rented would be adequate; he wouldn't be here long anyway. Just enough time to complete the business he intended to conduct. From what he had already seen, his new neighborhood seemed to be a quiet place, pleasant even, and he had been assured by the owners of the home he had rented that Gordonston was a genteel neighborhood, where people kept themselves to themselves, and that nothing out of the ordinary ever really occurred. It was, of course, different from his own country and home. He owned a much larger house, and though he had neighbors, so big were the grounds of his home, he never encountered them. It was going to be odd living so close to others.

As he delved into the last suitcase, containing his personal possessions, he paused briefly and smiled as he removed photographs of his family. He lovingly wiped each framed picture with a cloth before placing them on shelves and the mantel piece above the fireplace. His wife, his son, his grandchildren, his brother and then last of all a photograph of his parents; a black and white image of happier times. People had often told him he resembled his mother, others told him he looked more like his father. He didn't know. He gently stroked his mother's face; she had been a beautiful woman, a kind and caring mother, and she would have been proud of him and the grandson she had never met.

His murdered mother, his murdered father, victims of one of humanities greatest tragedies, victims of a man hell bent on destruction, an evil man who had created a regime of terror and hate, a regime that had singled out his family and others like them, who had persecuted them, taken not only their possessions but their dignity, and, ultimately their lives. Six million — six million of his people slaughtered — interned in labor camps and then concentration camps, just as he had been, just as his parents and brother had. Anger welled up inside him, anger that had lived with him for many decades. He clenched his fist, causing the faded blue tattoo on his hand, the tattoo containing just numbers, to appear to become larger as the skin surrounding it made it appear to bulge and grow. He took a deep breath and closed his eyes.

He was eight years old when the Nazis arrived in his village. At first, they thought they would be safe, that they would not waste their time singling out who was and who was not Jewish. But there had not been any reprieve. His family had been singled out almost immediately, their home ransacked, what possessions they had, stolen, and then a few days later they had been transferred to the camp.

He could still remember the train journey, treated like

cattle and with hundreds of others transported like animals, afraid and unsure of the fate that lay ahead. There were rumors, rumors that he overheard the adults discussing, rumors that they were being sent east, merely being sent back to the countries of their roots. But then there were the other rumors, talk of a word he had never heard before — genocide — and impending certain death.

He had been separated from his parents and his younger brother the moment the cattle truck door opened, and they had been ordered to disembark by the soldiers, who kicked and spat at them. He had turned back to look inside the truck that had been his home for three days. Lifeless bodies of those who had not completed their journey lay strewn on the floor. He was afraid, confused, and now, alone.

He remembered the two lines; the soldiers and guards had separated the trainload of people into two separate lines; he did not know which line to join. He had spotted his parents, in the left line, with his brother, who was clutching his mother's hand. As he walked towards them, he was grabbed violently, a voice in a language he did not understand spitting out words and instructions pointing to the line on the right. He had managed to make eye contact with his mother, and she had mouthed the words "go" in his own language. He joined the line, which seemed to consist of younger men and boys older than he, not the line that contained his family.

Many times he had supposed that it was most likely the fact he looked older than his years that had saved him from the gas chamber that day. Though only eight, he looked older. He was strong, and bigger than most of the boys who had already had their bar mitzvahs.

He had been put to work immediately, and for the next three years he was transferred from one labor camp to another, never knowing if he would be selected for the 'other' line. He had suffered, as they all had suffered, but he had lived. The day the British soldiers arrived at the camp, after his tormentors and guards had fled, not before killing as many of the camp's prisoners as they could, he had been barely alive. Starving and weak, he had feigned death and hidden amongst a pile of corpses, corpses clad in the striped uniform they had been forced to wear.

He could never forgive them — how he hated those people for the murders they committed on behalf of that man — a crazed lunatic who had the power of life and death over millions. And for what? To single out those who were different, to blame others as an excuse for the failings of his own race.

He fell back into a chair and sighed. So, this was it, Gordonston. He had arrived, and at last he could avenge those he loved. An eye for eye, a tooth for a tooth. He retrieved another picture frame, raising it to his mouth he kissed the face that adorned the photograph. “Soon, very soon,” he whispered.

# CHAPTER ELEVEN

"So how are the driving lessons going, Betty?" asked Heidi Launer, as she took a bite of Betty Jenkins's delicious fried chicken, closing her eyes as the tender chicken and crispy coating entered her mouth. It was, as always, fabulous.

"Why just fine, Miss Heidi," replied Betty as she put on her coat, preparing to leave her employer for the evening and return to her own home.

"Well, you are a braver woman than me. I cannot remember the last time I drove a car. I really admire you. I think my buying you a car and helping you get a driving license will not only help me but you also."

Betty nodded her agreement. A few weeks earlier, Heidi had had the notion that it would be beneficial if her housekeeper had a better means of transportation than just the city bus. It would benefit her to have Betty on call, as well as working her normal hours. It seemed common sense to buy a car for her use, and of course pay for lessons to enable her to drive it. It wasn't as if she couldn't afford it. Betty had jumped at the chance of learning to drive. She knew that her employer's motives were more self-serving than good-natured, but that hadn't deterred her enthusiasm to learn. And though the car would not be hers, Heidi had promised her that she could use it whenever she liked, and that of course she could use it for her own personal use. Heidi was getting older; she knew it would only be a matter of time before she would have to rely on Betty, not just for cooking and cleaning, but to provide her care as her age advanced. Betty, though she didn't know it yet, would not only be Heidi's housekeeper, but would also become her caregiver, Heidi always planned ahead.

Once Betty had departed, not before clearing her employer's plate, Heidi retired to her living room. Fuchsl lifted his head from his dog bed, acknowledging his mistress's entrance, and wagging his tail, before lowering his head, apparently disappointed she was not holding his leash. So, thought Heidi, the election was tomorrow. As she peered from the living room window, her eyes shifting to her neighbor's lawn. She knew who she wouldn't be voting for, even if the odds were he was going to win anyway, and by all accounts by a landslide. Elliott Miller, the fraud and liar, still alive and, despite numerous calls to her son Stephen, no explanation as to why her proposed contract on the man who had stolen from her family, masqueraded as something he was not, had not been carried out. Nor had there been any word about the money she had paid to have him killed. Her son had explained he was trying his best to get her news, to find out what was going on, or in this case, what was not going on, but he had few answers. Apparently it wasn't just Heidi who was disappointed; many of her son's criminal clients had also expressed their frustration at the lack of activity by this so called 'organization'. It appeared they had simply vanished.

What a complete waste of time, she thought. If you need something done, do it yourself. That was the problem with things these days. If only she had just killed Elliott herself. She had had the opportunity many times, and despite her age, it wouldn't have taken much to sneak up behind him and put a bullet in the back of his head, though of course she would have preferred to shoot him between the eyes, so he could see it was she who was his executioner. She would have reveled in the pleasure of his seeing her smiling face as the last thing he ever saw, unaware of the reason his neighbor was killing him. And who would even suspect her anyway? Who would have suspected an old lady; no motive, no witnesses, and no proof? Heidi regretted ever trusting her business with her son, and his so called 'connections'.

What sort of Mayor would he make anyway? A Jew? What were the people of Savannah thinking? Even a black Mayor was better than one of *those* people. Maybe they just didn't know, maybe they didn't even care. Idiots. And now another one had moved into the neighborhood? The Polish one, who had rented Brenda Carter's house on Henry Street. She shuddered. What was happening to Gordonston? It was becoming infested. Soon they would be everywhere, then God forbid interbreeding, eradicating those who were purebred. She closed her eyes. So many of these interracial marriages. Soon, if someone didn't stop it, it would be she and her kind who would be the minority, the pure blooded races wiped out, by what? Love? A more tolerant generation? It was utter nonsense. If *he* had had *his* way there would be none of 'those people'. The world would have been a better place, everyone in their place, none of these terrorists fighting over that piece of dirt called Israel. It wouldn't even have existed. There would be no war. There would be harmony; the world led by the master race. If they had succeeded, there would have been order, discipline, cures for diseases, science would have progressed further. China and India the best economies in the world? Not if they had had their way. Crime would have been dealt with correctly, not that there would have been any crime, as those who ruled would have ruled with an iron fist, would have ensured that there would have been no descent into chaos. If only they had stopped to think. What *they* were trying to achieve was the right thing to do. Heidi calmed herself, before she worked herself into a frenzy. The world had had its chance, and it was their loss.

Heidi suddenly felt tired, no doubt brought about by her hatred of, and anger at, the world. Not for one minute did Heidi consider that she was wrong, that her beliefs were abhorrent, that the philosophy, indoctrinated into her as a child, was evil. As far as she was concerned, it was they who were evil, as proved by the actions of her neighbor. Not for one minute did Heidi consider the innocent, the lives lost nor the pain suffered by millions. As far she was concerned, they had deserved it.

The old woman felt that an early night would be in order. She commanded Fuchsl to follow her up the stairs to her bedroom, and once again the dog appeared disappointed that he was not to be taken for at least a quick walk. Sulkily he followed his owner. As she passed her 'secret room' she paused, gently caressing the door knob, her past, her glorious past, memories and relics of an ideal that she worshiped, an ideal that she could only hope would one day rise again. She suddenly shuddered, a cold chill engulfing her body. What if her secret ever got out? What if she was ever exposed? What then? She would be shunned, maybe even worse. She had heard of people being deported to whence they came for having been a member of the party. They would take everything, her home, her money and of course her reputation. She couldn't imagine the uproar if anyone ever entered her secret room, or even had any idea about her past. All her secrets, all her things, her beliefs. Betty would surely resign, she would be thrown out of The Gordonston Ladies Dog Walking Club, people would not understand. No, the thought was simply abhorrent to her.

# CHAPTER TWELVE

Billy Malphrus enjoyed moments like this. He had the whole house to himself, apart from Paddy; whom he did his best to ignore. His Aunt Cindy had left earlier to cast her vote in the mayoral election, advising him, not for the first time that day that, "Elliott is going to win! Go, Elliott!" and to canvass on behalf of Elliott Miller at polling stations across the city. She had become a pivotal part of the campaign, according to her at least, and she would be gone for the whole day. Billy had of course agreed with her that Elliott, if he did win, would owe his victory to Cindy, that he too believed he was the ideal candidate, and like Cindy, the people of Savannah would be just crazy not to elect him Mayor. The truth was Billy didn't care, he wasn't bothered who won the silly election; it meant nothing to him. Who cared about Savannah? It was a small, boring town, filled with uppity rich people with an obnoxiously high opinion of themselves. Not to mention a certain amount of snobbery and unjustified self-importance. The only good thing about Savannah, thought Billy, was the fact you could walk the streets drinking alcohol from an open container, its St Patrick's Day parade and the fact that there was money to be made from its pompous and self-righteous inhabitants, many of those he classed as 'snobby', living in Gordonston.

He despised them. Rich, always in everyone's business, ignorant and spoiled. Self-important, self-serving and cocooned in their enclave of selfishness, they even kept that park to themselves, as if they had a divine right to it. Well, as far as Billy was concerned they were easy pickings, and he would feel not an ounce of remorse, once he mustered enough energy to begin his crime spree, focusing on the people of Gordonston. He would soon be inside their homes, taking anything he could find, and would they suspect him? No, of course they wouldn't. Why, he was the kind hearted nephew of Cindy Mopper; he wouldn't dream of ever stealing anything. He was a good boy, everyone knew it. Apart, of course, from Kelly Hudd, and she wasn't even here. Jerry Gordonston? Could she not have come up with something better? At least his false name, Count Enrico de Cristo, had been believable.

With Cindy out of the house, it gave Billy a chance to plan his next move, which involved breaking into the Hudd's empty house next door and stealing as many items as he could; clothes, jewelry, computers, televisions, everything. Then, he would pawn them, exchanging the stolen goods for what he craved more than anything else — stone cold hard cash. Billy, despite his ignorance, was a planner, and he decided the best way to formulate his plans was to write them down. He would write a checklist, listing those he would steal from, which stores he would use to pawn the stolen items and would begin recording details of his planned victims, including days and hours they worked, the time it would take him to effectively take as much as he could and which of their possessions he would make a priority. Top of his list was Kelly, second would be his aunt's friend Heidi, then maybe he would even target Elliott.

He needed a pen and some paper, to begin compiling his notes, and he reckoned the most likely place to find the implements he needed to put his plan into writing were probably in his aunt's desk, the one in the den, where her computer sat. As he rummaged through his aunt's desk drawers, in his search for a pencil or pen, he stumbled upon something that immediately peaked his interest. It was an envelope, an envelope he knew he had to open, and its contents he had to read. With curiosity taking a hold of him, he removed the envelope from the drawer, opened it and began to read the document inside it:

LAST WILL AND TESTAMENT OF

CINDY HELEN MOPPER

STATE OF GEORGIA

COUNTY OF CHATHAM

I, Cindy Helen Mopper, a resident of Chatham County, being of sound and disposing mind and memory, do make this my Last Will and Testament, hereby revoking and annulling all other wills and codicils heretofore made by me.

BURIAL AND FUNERAL EXPENSES

I desire and direct that my body be buried in a regular manner, suitable to my circumstances and condition in life, and a suitable memorial erected, the cost of my burial and memorial to be paid out of my estate.

BEQUEST OF ESTATE

*I give, bequeath, and devise to BILLY ULYSES MALPHRUS, all of my property, both real and personal, of every kind and description, wherever situated, whether now owned or hereafter acquired, including the rest, residue, and remainder, in fee simple.*

*In the event BILLY ULYSES MALPHRUS, does not survive me, or we die simultaneously, then I give, bequeath and devise all my property, including the rest, residue, and remainder of my estate to THE GORDONSTON RESIDENTS ASSOCIATION, in fee simple.*

Billy took in a sharp intake of breath and his eyes widened. This changed everything. This was an unexpected turn of events. So he would get everything, everything when she died? Everything! The house, the money and the good Lord only knew what else. He would never have to work again. He would be rich beyond his dreams. He wouldn't need to steal, con, work crappy jobs just to get by. He would have money, lots of it, as long as they didn't die together, or him before her, but what were the chances of that? He could ignore the second part, the bit about the stupid Residents Association getting their already rich hands on anything. And no mention of having to care for her stupid dog either. No clauses, nothing preventing him from selling her assets, her house included, and nothing stopping him from having Paddy put to sleep. He could sell this place and move to somewhere exotic, somewhere cool, maybe Miami, even Las Vegas. Billy's mind was racing: he could travel, without having to pretend to be someone he wasn't; he could live like a king. Women would flock to him; he could buy a sport's car, designer clothes, and he could do anything he wanted. Already he was making plans, spending his inheritance in nightclubs, living in a luxurious apartment; he would be a jet setter; he would be a playboy, and he could actually really live like his alter ego, Count Enrico de Cristo; a yacht maybe? This was all he had ever dreamed about: wealth, money, possessions and an easy life.

Just as quickly as Billy's elation and euphoria had begun, it subsided. His heart sank and thoughts of casinos, gorgeous women and boats evaporated as quickly as they had materialized. Of course he didn't have it yet. He would have to wait, and God only knew how many years. His aunt was a healthy active woman and had years ahead of her. She was never sick, and, knowing his luck, she would live to be a hundred. The chances were he could never keep up his act; the act of being the loving nephew, the charitable and kind hearted boy who adored his Aunt Cindy for much longer. He was already finding it difficult to put up with her constant talking, her constant open displays of affection towards him, and he was finding it even more difficult to keep up with his own lies. It would only be a matter of time before he blew it and Cindy found out what he was really like. And what if that Kelly showed up? Began spilling the beans, told Cindy about his antics in Paris? That, supposed Billy, was more likely to happen than him blowing it himself. All it would take would be Kelly to reappear and he could wave goodbye to his money, his dreams, and any chance he had of living a stress and work free life. Once Cindy saw through his façade of lies and deceit, she would change her will, leaving it all to either her neighbors, or probably some stupid animal charity, maybe even to her stupid dog. No, he could forget the money and any inheritance. Billy folded up Cindy's last will and testament, put it back into the envelope and placed it back inside the drawer of Cindy's desk.

Billy stared at Paddy, sleeping on the rug in the den; he wanted to kick him. He wanted to take out his frustration on anything, and as Paddy was closest, he would do. He couldn't exactly tell on him. There were no witnesses; he could do what he wanted to Paddy. It was then Billy had a thought, and instead of kicking Paddy he sat down on the sofa. Another plan was forming in Billy's head. No witnesses. Of course. Billy couldn't wait for his aunt's money, nor could he afford to wait for Kelly to suddenly return and ruin everything. He could keep up the ruse, he was sure he could, if the payoff meant a big return, for a little longer. There was really no choice, quite simply, if his life was ever to improve, if he was ever to actually live, not struggle, then Cindy's life had to end.

That, though, was easier said than done. He considered several scenarios. For one thing, Cindy just "disappearing", which seemed to him to be a common occurrence in Gordonston, was not an option he could even consider. Even Billy knew that before any inheritance could be paid to any beneficiary the departed had to be pronounced officially dead, that it could take years before he received any money, and of course what money his aunt did have would be wasted by attorneys and who knew what else. And how could he make her disappear? Bury her in the park? Dump her body at sea? That would have meant he would have to have killed her first, something he was sure he could do, as long as it was quick, and not gruesome, but chopping up her body? Even handling a corpse sent shivers down Billy's spine. Billy, above everything, was a coward. Even though he knew, for him to get a penny of his aunt's money, before she lived until a hundred, he would have to do her in, the actual thought of clubbing her to death, choking her or even touching her scared him. What if he did it wrong? What if he buried her alive, and she dug herself out of any place he had entombed her?

Maybe he could get somebody to do it for him. Maybe he could hire somebody to break into the house, bash Cindy on the head, and then someone could find her later. He would of course have an alibi; he wouldn't even be in Savannah when the dastardly deed was done. Billy dismissed the idea from his mind as quickly as it had formed. How the hell did you even go about hiring a hit man? It wasn't as if they had websites or were dispensing flyers advertising their services. Hit men and professional killers only ever appeared in stupid movies, or even more stupid books. No, Billy would have to do this himself. Maybe, he thought, he could stage a fake burglary himself, club his Aunt Cindy to death, while pretending he was somewhere else.... No... he didn't have the stomach for it. And what if she didn't die? She would identify him and he would spend the rest of his life in prison.

Paddy stirred on the rug and stretched. That damn dog, thought Billy, always digging in the trash, eating anything and everything thrown at him; it was a miracle the dog had not eaten anything to make him sick. Maybe Billy would feed him something to make him ill, just to teach him a lesson.

Billy smiled. Of course, it had been staring him in the face all along.

# CHAPTER THIRTEEN

"Who is that?" asked Heidi, as the gate to the park creaked open.

Carla and Cindy turned to face the entrance to the park just as an old man, dressed in a suit, his hair slicked back, entered. "Is he a resident of Gordonston? I have never seen him before. What does he think he is doing? This isn't a public park," continued Heidi, before her friends had a chance to even contemplate her first question.

"Oh, I do believe that is the lovely gentleman who has moved into Brenda Carter's house on Henry Street, the one I told you about," replied Cindy. "From Peru, no Poland, or somewhere like that. I am going to call him over. Let's introduce ourselves."

Before either Heidi or Carla could agree or object to Cindy's idea, their friend began waving her hand, attempting to attract the attention of their new neighbor.

"Hello, over here," shouted Cindy. "Yes, you, you there by the gate."

The old man looked around; the woman shouting and

waving obviously was shouting and waving at him. He began walking towards the trio of women sitting at the picnic table, who he noticed all had red plastic cups on the table in front of them.

"He is coming over," said Cindy excitedly. "Isn't it great to meet new friends? He looks dapper, just the sort of person this place needs," she beamed. Once again, neither Carla nor Heidi replied.

"Good afternoon, ladies," said the man as he approached the picnic table where the ladies sat. "I hope I am not intruding on your afternoon," he said politely, his accent thick, though his English was perfect. He offered his hand first to Heidi, then to Carla and Cindy in turn and then bowed his head.

"No, please join us," said Cindy with a welcoming smile. "I'm Cindy," she said, and turning to her friends, she said, "and these are my friends Heidi and Carla."

The old man nodded and continued to smile. "Ah, yes, the famous 'Dog Walking Club' – I was told many things about you. Good things, from the lady whose home I have rented. I am told you are the ears and the eyes of the neighborhood. I am Stefan, and I recently moved into a quite beautiful home on Henry Street." He took a deep breath and sucked in the warm afternoon air. "I love this weather, this temperature, we are lucky, no? To have at our disposal such a beautiful park?"

It was Heidi who spoke first. "Well, yes we are, as long as we keep the riff-raff out. You know, those that don't belong." She took a sip of her cocktail and eyed Stefan suspiciously.

"It is good to know then that you are here," replied Stefan, "watching out for the so called 'riff-raff' and those who don't belong. I feel safe and secure in the knowledge that this place is so well protected."

Heidi detected sarcasm in the man's voice, but ignored it, and she doubted that either of her friends had even noticed. She was, however, too busy trying to pinpoint his accent to respond to his rudeness. European, obviously, eastern most definitely.

Carla spoke next. "Stefan, if I may call you Stefan, your accent, it is very interesting, very exotic if I must say. Where are you from?"

Cindy smiled to herself. That was Carla, flirting as usual, but when before Cindy would have been angered and outraged by her friend's obvious flirtation, she now saw it as harmless, as no longer a threat to her, and anyway, this one was too old for her, let alone Carla. He was more Heidi's type.

"I am from the Ukraine," replied Stefan. "Kiev. Have you ever been?" he asked Carla, briefly glancing at her chest, before regaining eye contact.

Carla smiled. Even this old man found her attractive, just like them all. She hadn't failed to notice him looking at her fake boobs.

"I haven't," replied Carla. "I have never been to Europe. I would like to though, one day. Heidi has been though, haven't you?" said Carla, indicating towards Heidi.

"You have been to Kiev?" asked Stefan, staring at Heidi, and not for one minute averting his gaze to her chest, or any other part of her body.

"No, I haven't. I have, of course, been to Europe, many, many times," answered Heidi coldly.

"She is from Europe," added Cindy. "Where is it you are from again?"

Heidi wasn't at all pleased that her two friends appeared to be diverting all attention towards her. Were they match making? Trying to somehow set her up with this stranger? Heidi didn't like questions, especially questions about her past.

"Austria," replied Heidi. "I was born in Austria, Vienna, if you must know."

"Vienna," said Stefan, still staring directly at Heidi. "I hear it is a lovely place, lovely people, so I am told."

Heidi did not reply. Still staring back at Stefan, she took a swig of her beverage.

Stefan once again smiled and ceased focusing his attention on Heidi. He took a seat at the picnic table next to Cindy and addressed the group collectively.

"My wife died a year ago. She had been sick for some time. Since then I have been alone. It is cold in Kiev, very cold, and my old bones don't appreciate the ice and snow these days. So, I seek out warmer climates. I travel much, but this is my first time in your beautiful country. I am only here for a month, maybe two, then I will continue my journey, renting homes for short times as I see the world, meet new friends, and, like today, two charming 'Southern Belles' and one," he turned to face Heidi, "Bavarian Beauty."

Carla and Cindy looked at each other and smiled. *What an absolutely charming and delightful man,* thought Cindy. So polite, so sophisticated; what a great addition he would be to Gordonston.

Carla also found Stefan charming. Maybe he was a little older, maybe he wasn't her type, but there was something about him she liked. Carla had the ability to sniff out wealth, and she could, by his expensive suit, his expensive watch and the way he spoke, tell that this newcomer had money. Maybe her investment in having a boob job would pay off again.

"Do you have any children?" asked Carla, edging a little closer to Stefan, a move that did not go unnoticed by Cindy and Heidi, who both raised their eyebrows skywards.

"A son, a son I no longer see," replied Stefan, a brief hint of sadness in his voice. "And ladies, may I ask, are there three lucky men waiting for you all at home when you finish…," he looked at the three plastic cups, "…whatever it is that you are doing?"

"Walking our dogs," snapped Heidi, once again noting the sarcasm in Stefan's tone. "We are walking our dogs," she repeated, as she sat, taking a sip of her gin and tonic.

"How delightful," replied Stefan. "Ah, over there, I see them, such elegant animals," he said pointing towards Fuchsl, Paddy and Walter, who were playing chase through the trees.

"If only we humans were more like dogs. They hold no grudges, no bad thoughts. Such pleasant creatures," he added as he returned to addressing the group as a whole.

"Well, I have taken up far too much of your time already. Please, continue your dog walking. I am sure we will run into each other again. Ladies, I bid you a good afternoon." Stefan stood from the picnic table and bowed his head. He then took Cindy's hand and kissed it, before gently taking Carla's hand and also kissing it. Both Cindy and Carla could hardly contain themselves. Such a gentleman. Stefan then took Heidi's hand and raised it to his mouth. "If I may?" he asked.

As he raised her hand to his mouth, Heidi noticed something on his hand – a faded tattoo. Heidi immediately knew what it meant. Suddenly a sense of dread engulfed her. The tattoo. The mark of the concentration camp. He was a survivor. One of those who had escaped, one of those who had not been cleansed. Heidi, for a brief second, froze, her eyes firmly affixed on Stefan's tattoo. Her mouth was open, as if she was trying to speak, but her words could not leave her mouth. Heidi quickly averted her stare and regained her composure. She stared at the old man, her eyes meeting his, as if locked together by an invisible glue. His blue eyes seemed to pierce her skull. And was that a smirk across his face? He let loose her hand, after gently kissing it, and continued gazing into her eyes, and Heidi had the unnerving feeling he was gazing into her mind, into her soul.

"I am sure we will all get to know each other very well," said Stefan, who, though addressing all the ladies, seemed to be directing his comments towards Heidi, "very well indeed. I am sure in no time we will all become firm friends."

He once again flashed a smile at both Carla and Cindy, bowed his head again and made his way towards the park gate. As Stefan departed, Carla took a sip of her drink before speaking.

"What a lovely man," she said, "and I expect he is worth a fortune. Did you see his watch? That watch was one of those fancy Swiss things; they cost thousands."

"Oh, he is charming. Just what Gordonston needs, some class and sophistication," added Cindy.

"I think he took a shine to Heidi, don't you?" said Carla, nudging Cindy.

"Oh, I do. He could barely take his eyes of her. I think someone has got a new admirer."

Heidi frowned, and took a large gulp of her drink. She was shaking, and she hoped that her friends had not noticed. It appeared that they hadn't.

"I assure you," said Heidi, "he is not my type, not my type at all. In fact, I found him quite disgusting."

Carla and Cindy laughed, assuming that Heidi was of course joking.

"I am not feeling well," said Heidi as she stood from the picnic table. "Fuchsl," she shouted. "Fuchsl!" she shouted again, this time virtually screaming. Fuchsl turned his head towards Heidi, and as fast as he could, yielded to his mistress's command.

"Why, Heidi, whatever is the matter?" asked Carla, concerned for her friend and her sudden change of mood.

Heidi did not reply immediately; she seemed to be in a trance and did not even notice Fuchsl heel to her side. After a few seconds the trance-like expression that had engulfed her face disappeared and she smiled. "Oh, sorry, ladies, I just feel a headache coming on. Just irritating me, that's all. I am sure I can get rid of it, somehow or another."

"Well, it is getting late. Maybe it is time we all called it a day," said Cindy, genuinely concerned that her friend was sick. "I will walk with you to make sure we find something for your pain. Is Betty there today?"

Heidi rebuffed her friend's offer. She would be fine. Carla and Cindy still had half their cocktails to drink, and she would be okay, it was just a headache.

"Well, you take care, honey," said Carla as Heidi rose from the picnic table. "If you need anything, just holler."

Heidi nodded, indicating that she would indeed 'holler' if she needed anything.

As she made her way to her home, a few hundred yards from the park, with Fuchsl following behind, Heidi scowled. How on earth did he know?

# CHAPTER FOURTEEN

"The results are in... you won!"

Elliott Miller punched the air in delight and hugged the bearer of this euphoric announcement.

"Thank you, Harold, thank you. I couldn't have done it without your help, everyone's help, Cindy too. You have no idea what this means to me."

Harold Burns, one of Elliott's closest friends and official campaign manager for his mayoral run, shrugged. "It was easy, Elliott. My God you deserved it. It is about time this city had a decent Mayor. This is your moment and it is all down to you. Now, get ready. The press want a statement."

Elliott nodded and composed himself. If only Thelma had been alive to see this. She would have been so proud, elated that her husband had achieved his goal.

"One minute, let me call Spencer and Gordon in Los Angeles, I promised them I would let them know as soon as the results were in."

"Of course," replied Harold. "I will let the rest of the team know. Cindy especially, she has been calling practically every five minutes."

As Elliott called his step-sons, and Harold called Cindy, news of Elliott's win was already flowing through Savannah. Though the election had occurred the previous day, a recount had been ordered before any result would be announced, because the votes had been double those cast in the previous election, and the margin of Elliott's victory so vast, that the election board had first thought that some sort of error must have occurred. It had been a landslide victory, unprecedented in turn out and size. They had to be cautious.

Elliott had been nervous, unsure as to why no announcement had been made on the day of the election, but Harold had assured him, in fact promised him, that from all what he had heard, it was due to the fact that the vote counters had simply not been able to keep up, that it wasn't even a close run election. He had been right.

The next few hours were like a whirlwind for Elliott. It seemed he had shaken hands with half of Savannah and had his picture taken a thousand times. He smiled, grinned, raised his champagne class, had his back slapped and received numerous kisses on the cheek from countless supporters, most of them female. He had done it. Months of hard work had paid off. Now he could start doing what he had promised. He would be the best Mayor the city had ever known. He would get things done, improve the quality of life for everyone. What once had been a divided city would unite. There would be prosperity for all; he would put Savannah back on the map.

He made his acceptance speech, which was greeted by cheers and whoops of delight, the loudest cheer coming from Cindy Mopper. Elliott reiterated his campaign promises, and stated that his priority would be to combat the rising crime rate in Savannah. He would make the streets safe, increase the police department's budget, and recruit more officers. He also promised that he would bring more business to Savannah to ensure that the city would once again regain its reputation as a location for major conferences. He would give incentives to tourist-based businesses, to improve facilities, to fix the city's parking problem. Things were going to get better.

The crowd loved his acceptance speech. Even his opponents admitted that Elliott had the one thing they didn't; charisma. He was also a great speech giver, and the sincerity in his voice when he spoke was mesmerizing. He would take up his post officially in thirty days, giving the current incumbent time to clear his desk and hand over power. Power; that is what Elliott had now, and as he stood at the podium, thanking all who had voted for him, promising those who hadn't that he would also serve their needs, he couldn't help but remember the passion and the devotion he had witnessed all those years ago, where he had seen how the power of speech, the power of the ability to convince others to your way of thinking through words, had so impressed him.

All those years ago, watching Kurtz, or whoever he really was, putting his views across to the people of Buenos Aires, how he had the crowd hanging onto his every word.

Elliott Miller scanned the crowd, his supporters, press and the media. He sought out Cindy and winked at her. Cindy thought she would faint. Could this be it? Would he now see her as a potential wife? Would Elliott, now that he had achieved his goal, propose to her, maybe even now, as he made his acceptance speech?

Cindy pushed the thought from her mind. This was Elliott's day, and in a way, Thelma's day also. She couldn't wait though, to get home and tell Billy. Tell Billy that Elliott had won, confide in her nephew that maybe now, now that the election was over, Elliott and she may become a couple. It was the next natural step, no distractions, no pressure, just happiness.

As Elliott made his speech, and Cindy fantasized about the future, Heidi Launer shook with anger as she watched the local television channel's live broadcast of Elliott's speech. She stared at her television screen, her face distorted with hate. What was happening? Elliott Miller though, was not her biggest concern. She had other fish to fry, and Elliott would have to wait; she needed to protect herself before attacking him.

At the same time as Heidi scowled at her TV screen, Carla Zipp stared at hers.

Maybe now, she thought, Elliott would do the right thing, and propose to her friend. She felt nothing but joy, not just for Elliott, but for Cindy. How silly that Cindy had seen her as a threat, how preposterous a notion that she would ever come between Elliott and Cindy. Cindy was her friend, her best friend, and she, as much as Cindy, hoped that the Elliott and Cindy would eventually become a couple. This was as much Cindy's day as it was Elliott's, thought Carla.

Detective Jeff Morgan was also watching Elliott's speech, which was playing on the TV in the precinct. As his colleagues nodded their concurrence with Elliott's comments about crime rates and extra money for the police department, he did not comment.

Billy Malphrus, despite promising his aunt he would be watching Elliott's speech, did not even have the television turned on. He was too busy daydreaming about yachts, fast cars and a wallet full of cash.

Veronica Partridge was also not watching Elliott's speech. She was at that precise moment taking her expensive brand new SUV for a spin, heading to the mall to buy new shoes, a purse and toys for her daughter, unaware that her neighbor had become Mayor.

Kelly Hudd also had no idea that her former neighbor was now the new Mayor of Savannah, as she sat at her parent's kitchen table, a tub of ice cream in front of her, staring into space.

# CHAPTER FIFTEEN

Ignatius Jackson had many regrets, and as he lay on his bed, close to death; those regrets engulfed his final hours. He had taken a path in life that was not aligned to his beliefs. He had killed out of revenge. He had let bitterness, anger and hatred dictate his final years. He had been motivated not just by financial gain, but by a feeling that he had the power to dispense justice, to control the destiny of others. His medals, ribbons, so-called bravery and military service stood for nothing. That was not him. That was the Ignatius Jackson who had died seventeen years before, resurrected as a hateful and vengeful man, who had turned his back on goodness, God and his sense of right over wrong.

His lack of faith in justice had led him on the path which allowed him to dispense his own justice, allowed him to decide who would live, who would die. He knew, though, that, unlike a judge, he passed judgment and sentence on those unable to defend themselves, without trial, with no recourse to attorneys, for those he condemned did not have the opportunity to defend themselves. There were no trials, no mitigation, and no appeals.

What would May have thought? Would she have condoned his allegiance to the Organization? Would she have wanted him to exact revenge for her death? He doubted it. He also doubted she would be proud of the man she had once been honored to call her husband.

Soon, he knew, he would have to face a different kind of judgment. Despite abandoning his religion, he had once been a man of strong religious beliefs. Of course, those beliefs conflicted with his chosen path, and Ignatius had resigned himself to the fact that there would be no place for him in God's kingdom.

As death crept ever closer, the regrets overwhelmed him. For the first time in his life he felt genuinely scared. He felt fear, the fear of where his soul would spend eternity. He prayed for forgiveness. He begged God to forgive his sins.

He took a sip of water from the glass on the bedside table. At least he had sent the letter. Maybe he could do some good and save a life rather than end one. He just hoped the letter had reached its recipient in time, and that the recipient had acted on its contents. He would never know for sure, and he would never know for sure if the contents of his letter were even accurate. But he had sent it anyway.

Chalky, lying on the floor next to his master's bed, sat up on all fours and jumped onto Ignatius's bed. He curled his body onto Ignatius's lap, but before settling to sleep, he licked his master's face for the last time.

"Chalky," said Ignatius, "you have been a good friend." Ignatius Jackson closed his eyes for the final time, and peacefully, without any further words or thoughts, he died.

# CHAPTER SIXTEEN

"I would like to report my husband as a missing person. I haven't seen him in weeks; he hasn't called, and to be honest I am concerned." Veronica Partridge sounded worried as she spoke to the uniformed officer manning the inquiry window at the downtown Savannah police precinct. The officer behind the plastic screen looked at the woman opposite him and frowned.

"People go missing every day. If it hasn't been seven days, and he isn't a minor, what do you expect us to do?'

"Look, if you are not interested, or not even prepared to write a report, then get me someone who will. I will have you know I am a good friend of the Mayor, and yes, it has been longer than seven days, it's been over a month."

"Ok, ma'am - give me a minute, I will see if I can find you a detective," replied the officer, abandoning his post and heading to find someone who could deal with the attractive woman; claiming to be a good friend of the new Mayor.

Five minutes later, Veronica was beckoned through the locked door separating the public from the inner sanctum of

Savannah's Police Department, and was led by the uniformed officer to an open style office. There, she was directed to a cubicle; occupied by an overweight and bespectacled man who looked more like a pig than a detective.

"Detective Morgan," said the odd looking detective. "How may I help you?"

"My husband, Doug, Doug Partridge, is missing. I haven't seen or heard from him for over a month. I explained this to the officer at the front desk; he just vanished."

Morgan sighed, which didn't go unnoticed by Veronica Partridge. Here we go again, he thought, just like that other woman, the pretty blond one, whose husband had left her. He hoped that the woman in front of him, though attractive, but not as attractive as the girl who had reported her husband missing four months earlier, wasn't also a friend of Elliott Miller.

"And before you sigh again, I will have you know that I am a close friend of the Mayor," said Veronica, annoyed not only by the detective's obvious bad attitude, but also by the stench of offensive body odor that protruded from his chubby frame.

Jeff Morgan tried his best not to sigh again. How many women did the Mayor know? And how many of these good looking women had missing husbands? He forced a smile, and continued to speak.

"Okay. Give me a few details; age, description, social security number and the last time you saw him. Oh, and your address."

Veronica duly gave the detective Doug's age, date of birth, social security number, description and their address. Morgan, as she spoke, duly wrote the information he was receiving into his notebook, often raising his hand to indicate that Veronica was speaking too fast, that she needed to slow down.

"Okay. Kinzie Avenue," said Morgan. "Where is that exactly?"

"Gordonston," replied Veronica.

"Gordonston?" repeated Morgan.

"Yes, Gordonston," confirmed Veronica. "Why, is that an issue?" she said, having noted the hint of surprise in Morgan's voice.

Morgan scratched his head before replying. "No, not an issue, just I had another woman report her husband missing. She also lives in Gordonston, quite recently actually. She is a friend of the Mayor's also. Do you know the Hudds? Kelly and Tom?" he asked Veronica.

"Vaguely," replied Veronica. "I heard he had left her. Not sure why; she is gorgeous," she paused. "So is he actually missing?"

Morgan put his pencil to his mouth and tapped it against his lips before speaking again. He didn't reply to Veronica's last question. "Did you and your husband have any marital problems? Was there any problem in the marriage? You know, another woman, another man maybe?" Veronica shook her head. Morgan continued tapping his pencil against his lips.

"Look, we have a two year old daughter. There is simply no reason why he would vanish. Maybe things were tight and we had money problems, but I recently came into an inheritance. Things were looking up, so there is simply no reason he would just leave. No, something has happened to him. I know it. And as for another man? How dare you."

Morgan stretched his legs under his desk before speaking again. "I am sorry. I just needed to ask, you know, just trying to get the facts. Have you spoke to his friends? His family, his colleagues?"

Veronica shook her head. "He hasn't got any friends. He is from England, and he didn't have a job. He spent his time at home, looking after our daughter, well, until I got the inheritance money that is, then he was concentrating on writing a book."

The detective nodded as if he understood. "We will keep a

look out for him. If you have any recent photos of him, please can you get them to me and we will do what we can. To be honest, that won't be a lot. Your friend the Mayor has us all working on cold cases right now, so we are a little stretched, but I promise you, we will do our best. Maybe he is back in England?"

Veronica shrugged and rose. As she had expected, there wouldn't be much the police could do. She shook Morgan's hand and took the card he offered her.

"Hold on," said Morgan as Veronica stood to leave, "I think you dropped this." Morgan leaned beneath his desk and retrieved a stuffed toy. A small furry rabbit that had fallen from Veronica's purse.

"Thanks. It's my daughter's. She would be devastated if she lost it. It's her favorite toy," said Veronica, as she took the stuffed animal from Morgan.

Morgan leaned back in his chair and smiled. Case solved. Two cases solved in fact. It was obvious. Neither Tom Hudd nor Doug Partridge were missing persons and neither of them had run off with other women. They had run off together. Obviously they knew each other, and obviously they were lovers. Morgan, if he could have, would have patted himself on the back. An obvious case of two men falling in love and unable to face their families and admit that they were closeted homosexuals, not that Morgan thought there was anything wrong with that. Quite simply, these men had embarked on a clandestine homosexual affair. *It probably began*, thought Morgan, *when this Partridge fellow was at home bored beyond belief, writing his book, looking after his daughter*, which was, of course, woman's work. *He probably had a thing for hunky and good looking men in uniform, especially firefighters*. He imagined the pair of them meeting in the park and striking up a friendship. They were both relatively the same age, and apparently Hudd was an attractive man. Obviously, Partridge, being English and all, was probably gay, and had most likely gone to one of those schools where boys shared cold showers and wore shorts. Morgan had seen schools of that type on TV; no doubt Partridge had been the instigator, he had probably turned Hudd gay. Morgan had read somewhere that most attractive men had some sort of notion to become gay. He wasn't sure where he had read it. Probably on the internet. Odd, though, because he considered himself a very attractive man, and he was pretty sure he wasn't gay. Surely, supposed Morgan, this happened all the time, that's how it probably always happened. Two men, family men even, some even fathers, hiding their true feelings, living fake lives, hiding behind sham marriages. It happened in the movies, so why not in real life? In fact, the more he thought about it, Morgan was convinced this was the only plausible reason why these two men, who lived in close proximity, had disappeared. He had been wrong about Hudd leaving his wife because of her affair. No, Hudd was a closeted gay man, as was Partridge, and that, as far as Morgan was concerned, made perfect sense. He would not waste any more time searching for these two men, not that he had made much headway in his search for Tom Hudd. Let them enjoy themselves and live the way they please. *Good luck to them,* he thought. *Live and let live.*

Veronica Partridge returned to her car, parked in the police department's lot; her new expensive car. She turned on the ignition. She stared at her reflection in the rear view mirror. Her hairdresser had done a great job, and she felt she had deserved the treat. She looked at her manicured nails and admired them also. Then she smiled.

# CHAPTER SEVENTEEN

Police Chief Sam Taylor hated it whenever a new Mayor took office. They all made the same promises and it all involved reducing the crime rate, clearing up unsolved crimes, putting more officers on the street, which all added up to more pressure on him. Every new incumbent was the same. It wasn't until they realized there was simply no money in the city coffers and that there were no funds available for policing that they forgot their election promises. The Savannah Police Department simply did not have the manpower to combat the crime that occurred on a daily basis. Let alone investigate old crimes, crimes that were impossible to solve.

"Mayor Miller, if I may..."

"Elliott, please."

"Elliott, you must understand that the particular case you are referring to occurred over three years ago. There were no leads. There are still no leads. I assure you that my officers and this department did everything within our capabilities to investigate. Quite simply, it was a random street robbery that, though tragic, is not an uncommon occurrence in some, should I say, unsavory, parts of Savannah. Granted, they are not all fatal, but it was one of those 'wrong place - wrong time' sort of situations. I have the file here. I have spent the whole morning reviewing the details, as soon as you initiated this meeting. I am sorry but I just haven't the manpower to re-investigate a case that as far as I am concerned was a random mugging and is firmly closed."

From across the Police Chief's desk Mayor Elliott Miller nodded.

"I understand that. But the consequences of this killing had a major effect on the city. You do realize that this man was attending a conference, and that conference generated money for Savannah? You do realize that the organizers of the conference no longer even consider Savannah as a venue, due to the fact they deem Savannah unsafe? That is unacceptable. I agree with you when you say funds are tight, but Vladimir Derepaska was not just anybody. He was a major player for an international bank. He was worth millions. I understand it was a random mugging, and I understand that you investigated every plausible and possible lead; and I also understand that the chances of solving this crime are slim to none. That is not what I am asking. I want to send a message. I want potential visitors to understand that Savannah is a safe city and crimes are not simply left 'unsolved,' that we make a point of not letting anything go. This is a political gesture. If I can somehow convince big business that we are re-investigating this crime, they may, just may, decide that our city is a venue that can be trusted again to protect conference attendees. All I am asking is that you announce you have reopened the case, put a detective on it and leave me to spin the rest."

Taylor understood exactly what his new Mayor was asking. It was a public relations stunt. The murder and robbery of Vladimir Derepaska had indeed been big news, not only in Savannah, but in his home country. Robbed at gunpoint, and then shot for his expensive watch as he explored Savannah while attending an international banker's conference, held at the now seldom used Conference Center that overlooked the Savannah River downtown. He had strayed into the wrong area of town, more than likely lost, and as a result, lost his life. As the Mayor had said, the repercussions of his murder had led to the International Banker's Conference organizers choosing another venue for future conferences. Savannah, it seemed, in their mind at least, was not safe.

"You know, I doubt we will find any new leads, and you do realize the chances of actually solving this murder is probably less than one per cent?" said the Chief, scratching his head.

Elliott nodded. "I do. As I said, all I want is an announcement that the crime is being re-investigated, mention new leads. It is for the city. It is for Savannah. I am not saying put your best on it. Put any man on it, and I am not expecting an investigation. I just want people to believe there are new leads and that we haven't forgotten about it."

The police Chief sighed but concurred with Elliott's philosophy. "Look, I have one detective who I can assign to this. He isn't my best man, in fact he is probably my worst man, but if it is purely a paper exercise, then fine, I will go along with it." Sam Taylor understood politics, and as much as the next man, he loved his city, and he knew what Elliott had said made perfect sense.

Elliott smiled and rose from his seat and shook Taylor's hand. "Let me know who you are going to put on this, so he can liaise directly with me, if that's acceptable to you. I did meet one of your men, one of your detectives a few months ago, Morgan? Put him on it, he seems perfect."

Chief Taylor smiled; it was Morgan he had been thinking of. He detested the man. He was practically his worst detective, unpopular, reeking of body odor and constantly losing evidence, contaminating crime scenes and practically despised and regarded as a joke by his colleagues. Maybe by loading Morgan with this case, in addition to Taylor making the detective responsible for investigating missing persons a year ago, it would keep him occupied, maybe get him actually away from his desk. He was beginning to like this new Mayor.

"Sure, I will put him on it, not a problem," smiled Chief Taylor, who stood and shook hands with Elliott once more, who then promptly left and headed back to city hall. As he reached his car, he saw a familiar face. Veronica Partridge sat in her new car, admiring her hair in the rear view mirror. Poor woman, he thought, he had heard that her husband had run off back to England. Funny, he thought, just like Tom Hudd, just left, vanished, not even a word. He shook his head. Some men just don't know how lucky they are. Veronica was an attractive woman, who now even seemed more attractive with her new car, nice hair and fashionable clothes. Elliott shook his head. What he would give to have a woman like Veronica Partridge, or Kelly Hudd, at his side.

Chief Taylor took a sip of coffee and once again flicked through the Derepaska file on his desk. Pointless, he thought. It was a random mugging with no witnesses and no suspects. An utter waste of time, but maybe the Mayor had a point. He lifted up the phone receiver on his desk. "Send Detective Morgan to my office please.... "

# CHAPTER EIGHTEEN

Cindy Mopper had made a huge mistake and she knew it. Carla Zipp had no romantic feelings for Elliott Miller and never had. Cindy had totally misconstrued the situation and misread the signals, Carla must have been trying to snare another man and she probably had failed. The poor woman. Carla no longer dressed provocatively, no longer wore splashings of make-up nor did she any longer push out her false breasts, though Cindy did recall that Carla had made a point of flirting with Stefan the other day in the park. But that was a one-off, and anyway, Stefan wasn't Elliott.

Carla, whenever the Gordonston Ladies Dog Walking Club convened, dressed far more appropriately these days. Gone were the high heels and tight jeans. She hardly ever mentioned Elliott and she hardly ever commented about him. It was obvious that Carla found Elliott not the least bit attractive. Cindy surmised that Carla probably had joined some sort of dating web site, and had probably been the victim of some cad or bounder, who had probably been after her money. She had probably been going through a mid-life crisis. No doubt her odd behavior, acting the way she had, was a result of some ill-advised potential romance.

In fact, Carla had reassured Cindy, told her that she had no intention of ever trying to come between Cindy and Elliott. She had told Cindy that she considered Cindy her best friend, that it was actually her hope that Elliott and Cindy would eventually 'hook up'.

This had left Cindy with a huge problem. A devastating problem with unthinkable consequences, and a problem she could not seem to rectify. She had spent hours searching the internet, trying to find the remotest trace of the web site where, four months previously, she had paid and organized for her friend to be killed. Every day, for the past two months, for hours at a time, she searched for some way of contacting the organization, not for a refund, they could keep her money. No, she needed to cancel whatever they had in store for her best friend Carla.

But it was all to no avail. The web site had vanished, so there was nothing she could do. She had tried all she could. When she had organized the 'hit' on Carla, she had followed the instructions given on her computer screen to the letter, and those instructions had included removing all trace of the website. It was an impossible task, everything had been wiped.

She had tried the phone book, which had proved to be a complete waste of time also. The only exterminators she could find dealt with rats, mice and cockroaches.

She could not live with herself if something happened to Carla. She had acted in haste and out of jealousy, unfounded jealousy, and the consequences, the consequences were simply awful. Carla and Cindy, once Cindy had realized that Carla had no desires on Elliott, had become even closer. They had bonded and become firm friends; in fact, Cindy considered Carla her best friend, just as Carla considered her. The stress and burden of her guilt was too much to bear; the guilt she felt for her hasty and uncharacteristic actions was overwhelming.

She could only hope and pray that by some stroke of luck her contract was rejected. There had been, she recalled, a disclaimer stating not all contracts would be fulfilled, and there was the chance that nothing would happen… but what if it did? She couldn't warn Carla. How on earth could she begin to explain what she had done? Her only hope was that nothing would happen and that, hopefully, she had been the victim of a giant confidence trick, and this 'Organization' had never even existed in the first place.

# CHAPTER NINETEEN

Heidi Launer was furious. It was the second time that day she had spotted the old man's dog wandering the park, unleashed and unaccompanied, pooping everywhere and digging around. How dare Ignatius Jackson allow his dog free, and have full access to the park unattended? Obviously the dog was just being released into Jackson's yard and then crawling through the railings separating the yard from the park and having a free run of things. It was disgusting. She would make a point of informing Carla and Cindy of what she had seen, and no doubt another strongly worded letter would be drafted and delivered to the home of the offender.

Heidi had other things to worry about; a more pressing matter. Stefan to be exact. She had not failed to notice his tattoo and knew what it signified. Her mind had been racing from the moment she had met him a few days previously in the park. Was there a chance he knew her true identity? Was it just too much of a coincidence that, from nowhere, into her neighborhood appears this man, a so-called "holocaust" survivor? Not, thought Heidi, that there had been such a thing. It was all lies. Propaganda and fantasy, created by the Zionists to garner sympathy. She had her son Stephen do some investigating into the man, not that she had any faith in his abilities, especially after she had wasted all that money paying for Elliott to be killed, which of course hadn't happened.

Anyway, that aside, she really had no choice but to involve her son; he had the means and abilities to carry out background checks on anybody without inducing suspicion. Though he hadn't much to go on. She didn't even know his surname, and of course as he was foreign, so there would be no records of him in any system, not in the United States at least. Of course she had not been surprised when her son had reported back that there was no record of anyone called Stefan, who matched the description Heidi had given her son, on any database he could access. In fact, there was no record of him anywhere, no record of him arriving in the country. He was obviously not who he said he was, which begged the question, to Heidi anyway, what the heck did he want?

She could have called Brenda Carter, in whose house he was living. Maybe she had more details about Stefan. She couldn't rely on Cindy's information; it was always wrong or missing details. Heidi decided, though, that she wouldn't call Brenda. She hardly knew her anyway, and if she did start asking questions, there was nothing to prevent Brenda from calling her tenant and alerting him that one of his neighbors was poking about in his business. The last thing she wanted to do was let him know that she was on to him.

Heidi could only guess as to who he really was. He was probably one of those Nazi hunters, probably an agent of Israel. He was no doubt a spy; he was definitely here for her. He was going to expose her true identity; he was going to tell the world about everything. He was going to ruin her, destroy her life, or maybe worse. What if he was here to kill her? What if he was here for revenge? What was their saying, 'an eye for eye'? Well, she wouldn't give him or them the satisfaction. She would take matters into her own hands.

# CHAPTER TWENTY

Billy Malphrus stared at the plastic bag containing the rat poison he had just purchased from the hardware store. His plan was simple. He would make lemonade. Really, how hard could it be? He would then add enough rat poison to the concoction to kill his aunt. He would of course take precautions. He would pour the undrunk lemonade down the kitchen sink; he would remove all trace of the rat poison from the house. There was no way he could be caught. Billy would then inherit everything. He would sell the house, have the dog destroyed and spend his aunt's money having fun and living a life of unbridled luxury. She was old anyway, and it wasn't as if anyone would miss her. No, it was a simple plan, and that's how he liked things, nice and simple. He would of course act devastated and garner sympathy from everyone. Then he would move on, traveling the world, living the life he deserved, never having to work and struggle again.

If only his Aunt Cindy had maybe shared a little more. It was all well and good her taking him in whenever he needed it, and of course feeding him, and not to mention donating to his fake charities, but if she really cared for him she should have given him more money, maybe set up an allowance for him. She didn't need much, whereas he did. He needed fancy clothes, a fast car, and the opportunity to live life in the fast lane. He was sick of working dead-end jobs and then having to pretend to be other people. He wanted to actually be those people. Billy Malphrus was motivated by one thing, and it certainly wasn't hatred for Cindy, though he was growing to hate her. No, Billy Malphrus was motivated by one thing… greed.

The hardest part of this plan, thought Billy, would be making the lemonade. It would also cost money; lemons didn't grow on trees, he thought. So he had spent the morning researching recipes online. Once confident he could produce tasty lemonade, with of course the added ingredient of rat poison, he headed out once again, this time to the grocery store to purchase lemons, sugar and sprigs (whatever they were) of mint and rosemary to add an extra bite, and hopefully mask the taste and smell of the poison he would add. His plan was to make a few batches of normal lemonade, without the added poison. He and his aunt would drink it together, he would offer to make more and more, and then, when the time was right, he would add the poison to the concoction and leave it in the refrigerator. Cindy would surely help herself to it, sooner or later, hopefully when he was not there. He wasn't sure if he could actually stomach watching her splutter, throwing up, foaming at the mouth and then dropping dead in front of him.

# CHAPTER TWENTY ONE

Stefan sat quietly in his easy chair, a stern and serious look on his face. He had never been this close before, within virtual touching distance of his sworn enemy, or in this case, the closet living relative of his enemy. The pleasure he would get finally extracting revenge for the tragedy that befell his family would be worth everything; leaving his home country, traveling halfway around the world, living in this wretched hot place and this tiny house. He had never, in his wildest dreams, ever thought he would be so close. His family would be proud of him. Of course, it had cost him money, lots of it, obtaining the information he needed, but it was worth it, every single penny.

Out of habit he found himself stroking his tattoo as he contemplated his plan. He knew where she lived now, and he knew what she looked like. Of course, exacting revenge on the man directly responsible for the crime against his family was not possible, but this, at least, would restore his family's honor. Once again, 'an eye for an eye and a tooth for a tooth'. You could hide from your past, you could run from your past, but sooner or later, the past always catches up with you. Soon the past would catch up with her.

He rose from his seat, headed to his bedroom and reached under his bed, retrieving a wooden box. It had arrived earlier that morning, couriered from somewhere in Florida. He had purchased it online. He opened it and took out the silver Glock 19. He inspected the weapon. He had never fired a gun, but that didn't faze him. It would be a close up shot. He couldn't miss anyway. The gun was heavier than he had expected, which had surprised him. For some reason he had always thought a weapon like this would be lighter. He opened the second box, which lay next to the box containing the pistol. It contained six bullets, but he knew he would only need one. He lifted the weapon skywards, admiring its design. He stared at the gun, sunlight catching it, causing it to sparkle in his bedroom. He inspected it further and noticed the engraved "Made in Austria" imprint on the gun's handle. He smiled.

# CHAPTER TWENTY TWO

Kelly Hudd put her car into drive and reversed out of her parent's driveway. She turned left and followed the signs for Interstate 16. Driving to Savannah was a weekly ritual for Kelly, something she had done every week, without fail, since Tom left her. She would make the three hour trip, and then resume her search. Despite Detective Morgan's informing her that Tom was unlikely to be in Savannah, she hadn't given up the hope that maybe she would spot him, maybe just casually walking along a downtown street, maybe at the gym, maybe even in Gordonston. Every week though, her efforts were in vain. Often she would just park her car and sit in it crying. Sometimes, she would park her car opposite her increasingly deteriorating home and just quietly sob. Never once was she tempted to enter her former house. Many times, with Shmitty sitting beside her, Kelly supposing that he had no understanding of what was wrong with his mistress and why he couldn't just go home, she had just stared at the once happy home. Shmitty must also be missing Tom, she thought, and probably his runs in the park. She was, though, always careful to ensure that she was never spotted by any of her former neighbors, not that they would recognize her anyway, not now she had put on weight.

This trip, she had promised herself, would be different. She had booked a room at a motel and would this time really search for Tom. She would spend four days in Savannah before returning to her parent's home. She would not sit in her car and sob, she would not feel sorry for herself. This time she would actually search for him, night and day, everywhere, she might even force herself to go inside their former and abandoned house. She desperately wanted to see Tom; she needed at least an explanation, and she needed to hear it from him that it was over. Maybe if she did find him, she could reason with him, convince him she had been duped, maybe deny anything he had heard. Maybe there was a slim chance that this all could be fixed. With Shmitty in the passenger seat, she put her foot on the gas pedal and accelerated.

As she headed eastward, Kelly was not sure what she would even say to Tom, if she even found him. She had no defense for what she had done, for cheating on her husband, and of course the fact she had cheated on her husband with their neighbor's nasty looking nephew just made things worse. Kelly tried to put herself into Tom's position; what if he had cheated on her with a neighbor, someone not half as attractive as she? She would be devastated, embarrassed and would probably have done what Tom had done, just run away. She considered turning the car around and returning to Atlanta. Maybe it was best to let things be. Maybe Tom was justified in leaving her, and no denials or begging for forgiveness would ever convince him that he could trust his wife again.

What hurt Kelly most was that he hadn't even confronted her, never even mentioning the fact he knew, and had just left. Another question Kelly had, was of course, how had he found out? Had that sniveling little bastard next door told him? Had she somehow left a clue? Had someone from the hotel in

France called her husband, anonymously, out of spite? Maybe that receptionist, who was obviously sleeping with the concierge. Kelly dismissed the notion, it was as preposterous as her being a model, and Billy Malphrus being a count. No. It had to have been Billy Malphrus who had told Tom, since he was the only one who knew. If only they, whoever they were, had killed him as she had paid them to. If only she had acted quicker. If she had known this was going to happen, she would have done it herself, killed Malphrus, how she didn't know, but she would have found a way, maybe poisoned the little cretin.

# CHAPTER TWENTY THREE

"Chief, sir, please, why on earth are you giving me the Derepaska case? It is closed, finished. What can I do?"

Chief Taylor did not care much for Detective Jeff Morgan; he was overweight, lazy, a poor detective and suffered from offensive body odor. The fact that Morgan was now complaining about being given the Derepaska file actually gave Taylor a feeling of pleasure. Though he knew that this was merely a paper exercise, a public relations stunt, and that the street robber who had murdered the poor Russian visitor for his watch was highly likely to remain at liberty, he felt that was something Morgan need not know.

"Listen," replied Taylor, as he sat behind his desk, "I want this solved. I want you to dedicate your fullest efforts on solving this. Interview every known mugger, robber and potential suspect currently on file. Re-interview witnesses. Re-interview potential witnesses. I want your full concentration on this one."

Morgan shrugged. "Come on, boss, give me a break, why me?"

"Because you are my best man and this comes from the Mayor. He wants this re-investigated and solved, and his exact words to me were 'put your best man on the job' - you are that man," lied Taylor. "He also mentioned you by name, seems he thinks you are up to the task."

Morgan straightened in his seat and smiled. Wow, so the Chief thought he was his best man. Even the Mayor had spotted his potential. Well, if that was indeed the case, that put a whole new perspective on the situation.

"Well," said Morgan, his attitude and demeanor suddenly improved, "I have just recently solved a double missing person puzzle. Two fellas from Gordonston; ran off together, closet gays, put two and two together and worked that one out pretty quickly," he boasted.

"Good for you, Detective," said Chief Taylor, who did not have the remotest interest in any case or cases Morgan was working on. "See? That's why you are my best man. Despite what everyone says about you."

Morgan's smile vanished. "What does everyone say about me?" he asked, suddenly feeling deflated.

Taylor shrugged. "Sorry, slip of the tongue. I meant to say this is what everyone says about you, that you are my best man."

Morgan's smile returned and he stood up. "Leave it to me. If I can solve a double missing person case without even leaving my desk, then I am sure I can at least get somewhere on this."

Chief Taylor nodded. "Well, off you go then, go get 'em," he said, indicating with his hand that it was time for Morgan to leave. "By the way, the Mayor wants to talk to you. He wants progress reports. Take this." The Chief handed Morgan Elliott's card. "Call him, he wants to set up a meeting."

This was not the first time Morgan had been asked to work on a specific case by the Mayor. Four months earlier, Alderman Miller, now of course Mayor Miller, had accompanied Kelly Hudd when she had reported her husband missing. So the Mayor had taken a shine to him? And why wouldn't he? Everyone liked him, he was popular, and a fine detective. Maybe this could be the boost he needed, maybe a promotion was on the cards?

He would take the opportunity of updating the Mayor on the Hudd/Partridge case. He would let him know that case was well and truly closed. That would surely impress Miller.

"Why are you still here?" asked the Chief, staring at Morgan, who in turn was staring into space, a stupid grin covering his face.

"Sorry, I'm leaving now," he replied.

As soon as he left the Chief's office, Sam Taylor opened up his desk drawer and retrieved some air freshener. Screwing up his face, he sprayed his office with a refreshing scent of lavender before replacing it back into his drawer.

# CHAPTER TWENTY FOUR

"Oh, Billy, this tastes just wonderful," said Cindy Mopper as she took another swig of Billy's homemade lemonade. "You certainly are a man of many talents. That's why I just love you so darn much," she beamed as she finished off her glass.

Billy grinned and took a sip of lemonade; he had to agree with his aunt, it wasn't half bad. "Well, that's a whole jug we have drunk," he said. "I will be sure to make a fresh batch for tomorrow, and the day after. I kind of enjoy making it, but what gives me the most pleasure is that you enjoy it."

Cindy was ecstatic. She loved the fact Billy was here again in Savannah. Who could want for a better, kinder and loving nephew?

"Well, it is delicious," said Cindy as she collected the dirty glasses and placed them in the dishwasher. "Let me give you $10, so I can contribute to the ingredients. Please, it's the least I can do."

Billy stared at his aunt's back as she opened the dishwasher. Selfish horrible old woman, he thought, all I do for you and you offer me a measly ten bucks? *The sooner you die the better*, he thought. He was scowling. Cindy turned to face him and in an instant his smile returned.

"I just don't know how you do it," said Cindy with a smile. "You never cease to amaze me."

"You know it's nothing," replied Billy. "Anything for you. Nothing is too much trouble, you know that."

"I know, Billy, I know it. It is such a comfort to me knowing that as I get older you will be around. I hope so anyway. To maybe care for me on a more permanent basis. I would love you to live here permanently. We could come to some sort of arrangement. I am not getting any younger and, what with your experience caring for others, you would make an ideal care giver for me, you know, when I eventually need it."

The thought of caring for his aunt as she got even older appalled Billy. She had the audacity to ask him to feed her, clean her, and drive her around, as if he was some sort of home help? A servant? Was she mad? He stifled a smile. Not that it was ever going to happen anyway. She was not going to grow any older, and she certainly would not need any help.

"Wow, I would love that," lied Billy as he took a final sip of his lemonade; before placing the empty glass into the dishwasher. "Maybe I should consider it. It would be my pleasure to live with you, and of course Paddy. I love him as much as you do."

# CHAPTER TWENTY FIVE

Carla Zipp had given up on men. She was sick of them. Always lying, trying to use her. She had finally realized that she was better off without them in her life. She had devoted too much time and effort in believing that her looks were her best asset. For heaven's sake, she thought, she was 65, it was time she grew old gracefully and maybe followed the example of her friend Cindy. Cindy was happy, everybody liked her, and she wouldn't even harm a fly. She had that wonderful nephew and had grown old gracefully. If Carla could turn back time, she would have never let herself become infatuated with Tom Hudd. She certainly would never have slept with him. She did not, however, regret having him killed. He had deserved it. He had crossed the wrong woman, a woman already once betrayed by a cheating husband, he too now dead.

Enough was enough, there was no more dressing like a tart. She would act her age, there would be no more spending obscene amounts of money on make-up, clothes and ridiculous plastic surgery.

It had been more trouble than it was ever worth. Did she regret having Tom Hudd killed? Not at all, not one bit. Anyway, it was the past, and her only regret was poor Kelly. She hadn't hurt anybody, in fact she had been just as much a victim of Tom's deceit as she had. Carla had hoped that in time she and Kelly could have become friends, that she would join The Gordonston Ladies Dog Walking Club, that maybe she would meet a new man, move on with her life. Sadly, that had not been the case. Kelly's nervous breakdown had been common knowledge, according to Cindy anyway, who had made it common knowledge. The poor girl had been convinced Tom had left her. Initially Carla had been worried that Kelly had found out about her and Tom's fling, but it seemed Kelly harbored no such suspicion. It seemed Kelly blamed herself. That poor deluded girl, thought Carla.

Anyway, Carla had plans, new plans, and it involved rekindling an old romance. Gino had always been there for her; for over 40 years he had carried a torch for her. It had been thanks to him she had been able to exact her revenge against Tom. She now spoke to Gino every day. She was busy planning a vacation to see him in Las Vegas. Who knew where this could lead? Gino was not like the Tom Hudd's of this world. There were certainly no decent men in Savannah that was for sure. She sometimes felt sorry for her friend Cindy. Her infatuation with Elliott seemed to be taking over her life, it was as if it was the only thing she actually cared about. Carla obviously hoped the two would eventually marry, at least for Cindy's sake. She could only imagine what lengths Cindy might go to if anyone ever came between her and Elliott. She doubted though, unlike herself, that she would ever resort to murder. Not sweet old Cindy. There really wasn't anything that attractive about Elliott anyway, not in Carla's opinion, in fact, he was quite boring, thought Carla.

The old man, Stefan, now there was something about him Carla liked, but he was obviously too old for her, and anyway, he seemed smitten with Heidi.

# CHAPTER TWENTY SIX

Billy Malphrus had just finished preparing his latest batch of lemonade. He paused before adding the rat poison. There would be no turning back from this. His plan was simple, he would leave the jug in the refrigerator and sooner or later his Aunt Cindy would pour herself a glass, drink it and drop dead. Then he would inherit her fortune.

For the past five days he had been making jug after jug of the stuff, he and Cindy had shared each batch of the refreshing beverage. She wouldn't for one minute think that this latest jug contained poison. His plan was perfect.

There was one problem, thought Billy, he didn't want to be around to see his aunt die. Despite his disdain for her, and the fact he was planning her murder, he could not face watching her die. The truth was that he was a coward. The mere thought of watching his aunt gag and choke and then spasm in pain made him shudder. He would have nightmares for months. He could only imagine the look of horror on her face as she begged him to call an ambulance. No. He would try and be out of the house as much as he could from now on.

He would make a mental note not to drink any lemonade and just hoped that she drank it, sooner rather than later. He stared at Paddy, who had watched him prepare the toxic and deadly concoction. Billy picked up his leash and waved it in the air.

"Come on, Paddy, time for a walk."

The dog rose, his tail wagging, but Billy scowled at the confused animal, hung the leash back on the coat rack behind the kitchen door, laughed, and left the house.

*****

Cindy Mopper was worried. Her finances were worse than she had thought. The money she had spent in her attempt to have Carla killed had almost wiped out her life savings. She was virtually broke. She had met with the bank manager that morning. He had told her that despite her husband's pension, she would soon have to think about selling her home, and find a smaller place. Not only that, despite yet another day trying to contact the 'Organization'; it had proven fruitless. She just hoped that Carla would be okay. She was tired. She would head home, maybe have a glass of Billy's lemonade....

# CHAPTER TWENTY SEVEN

Betty Jenkins would not be attending to Heidi today. She was taking her final driving lesson before her test the following day. She had spent the previous day reminding herself of the rules of the road. She had already passed the theory part of the test, and she felt confident she would pass.

She peered out her window, just as her instructor pulled up in his car.

*****

Heidi had spent the day preparing for the inevitable. Soon she would be disgraced. It was only a matter of time before Stefan, or whatever his real name was, would either be exposing her, or worse, executing her. She had gotten her affairs in order, written a letter for her son Stephen, expressing her disappointment in his inability to find someone suitable to kill Elliott Miller. She put some cash in an envelope for Betty Jenkins, along with a letter of reference, and had spent the rest of the day gazing with admiration at her collection of Nazi memorabilia and her collection of books.

# CHAPTER TWENTY EIGHT

For three days Kelly Hudd had driven all over Savannah searching for Tom. She had visited the gym and no one had seen him. She had visited the fire station; again not a word from him. Maybe Detective Morgan was right, maybe Tom just didn't want to be found. She had mustered enough courage though to return to Gordonston, and it was here she sat, in her car parked opposite her old home. She fiddled with the house key and bit her nails. It would be simply heartbreaking for her to return to the home. She took a deep breath and closed her eyes and convinced herself to be brave, that sooner or later she would have to once again step inside her house. When she opened her eyes her blood ran cold.

It was him.

He was back. That nasty, home wrecking, lying, two faced scumbag con man that was Billy Malphrus. There he was, leaving Cindy's house. Kelly ducked down as he passed her car on the opposite side of the road, walking on the sidewalk. The rage and hatred within Kelly was ferocious. There was the root of all her problems, the reason Tom had left her, the reason she now weighed over 160 pounds and the reason her life was ruined. Shmitty stared at Kelly, no doubt sensing the latent rage that was emitting from his owner.

She watched as he headed eastwards. She switched on her car engine and turned her car around. She would follow him, and then, maybe she would confront him.

# CHAPTER TWENTY NINE

Betty Jenkins was doing just fine. Her driving instructor had told her she would have no trouble passing her test tomorrow, and this final lesson was going well. Her instructor, though, had a request. Could she possibly stop at the Piggly Wiggly grocery store on Skiddaway Road? He needed to pick up some milk? Betty had no problem with that; in fact, it would be good practice for her, as she often had to pick up groceries for Heidi from the nearest grocery store to Gordonston. It wouldn't be a problem at all.

# CHAPTER THIRTY

He had no problem finding a taxi cab. There was a line of them outside the arrivals hall. He checked his watch, he hoped he wasn't too late and that being back in Georgia wasn't a mistake.

"Welcome to Savannah," said the cab driver. "No luggage?" he commented as he entered the rear seat of the cab.

"No, none, just take me to Gordonston. You know where that is, right?" he asked.

The driver nodded.

# CHAPTER THIRTY ONE

Jeff Morgan had spent the whole day reading the old case file regarding the Derepaska murder, and he had gotten nowhere. He was ready to give up. He had gone through every scrap of evidence, including the original investigating officer's report and all statements. It was a complete waste of time. He was ready to go home, when he suddenly did a double take. It was a list of names. He picked up the piece of paper that had been previously hidden under a pile of other papers and examined it. It was a list of all the attendees at the conference. Not one of them had been interviewed or spoken to, as when the conference had ended all the attendees had returned to their respective cities or countries. However, one name stared back at him. Was it a coincidence? Could this be the same Doug Partridge whose wife had reported him missing a few days ago, the same Doug Partridge who had run off with his gay lover Tom Hudd? Surely not. But, maybe, just maybe it could be worth visiting Mrs. Partridge in the morning, just to see if there was anything she could add to the investigation.

He was tired in any case, his long lunch with the Mayor

had brought about afternoon fatigue, and though he had work to do, he decided to call it day. It was also that time of the week he took a shower.

# CHAPTER THIRTY TWO

Elliott Miller no longer opened the anonymous letters he received on a weekly basis. He now recognized the handwriting on the envelope, and every letter he had received just said the same things. 'I know what you did' or 'Thief' were the usual words which accompanied a tirade of hate-filled and anti-Semitic prose. He now just threw the unopened envelopes straight into the trash.

He had considered contacting the police, reporting the letters, maybe even, for once and for all, getting to the bottom of it, and discovering who his tormentor was, but that would have meant explaining about the children's books he had written, and maybe even trying to explain his encounter in Argentina years before, and about how he had plagiarized an old man's stories. An old man who may or may not have been the most hated and vile man in the history of the planet. The potential publicity and political fallout would be disastrous. He would either become a laughing stock, or worse, lose the trust of the people of Savannah. Who would want a man who had stolen another's stories as a Mayor? He could do nothing, and after all they were just letters, he doubted that the person behind them had any intention of carrying out the veiled threats.

As the new Mayor of Savannah, he had more pressing issues than the ramblings of a mad person and book's, long since forgotten. Number one on his agenda was the crime rate. Elliott wanted Savannah to be a safe place and a destination tourists and visitors could feel secure in. He respected Chief Taylor, and knew that he understood why Elliott wanted the Derepaska case re-opened and re-investigated, or at least the appearance that it was being re-investigated.

Despite his victory and his position, Elliott Miller was lonely. Though Thelma had been dead for over six months, he was still not used to the empty house, and he yearned for the companionship that a relationship would give him. He had, of course, considered Carla Zipp as a potential girlfriend, but he was relieved he had not pursued her. She was really too much; he felt she looked ridiculous, dressing the way she did, and for a woman at her age to have breast implants? What had she been thinking? While he did respect Cindy Mopper as a friend, a close friend, he simply did not find her attractive, and he could not see her as anything more than a friend, a good friend. Of course Cindy Mopper and Carla Zipp were not the only women in Savannah, there were others who had made advances towards him, but despite their being the same age as Elliott, or maybe a few years younger, he felt he deserved better, and why not? He was the Mayor, he was powerful, and he really could have any woman that he wanted.

He had arranged to meet Jeff Morgan for lunch at Leocci's Italian Trattoria, on Drayton Street, located close to the police precinct and his office. Morgan had been on time, and they had taken a seat outside in the courtyard.

"So, you actually ride that thing?" asked Elliott, as Morgan took his seat, removing his helmet.

"I love it. It is so economical, and quite fun to ride."

Elliott stared at the scooter Morgan had arrived on. He had seen quite a few of them lately, mostly being ridden by students. He was surprised that a detective would be riding one.

"It's a Vespa," said Morgan proudly.

"What is?"

"My moped, they are all the rage, much better than driving."

Elliott nodded, though he really wasn't interested in Morgan's opinion of mopeds, scooters or any other means of transportation.

The waiter brought over menus, and they both selected Risotto Frutti de Mare, one of Chef Roberto's favorites, according to the menu. Once the food arrived, Elliott spoke.

"So, Jeff, I am glad to have you working on the Derepaska case. It means a lot, though I am not sure if you will crack it, the point is that you are doing something, which means we, Savannah, haven't given up," said Elliott as he took a spoonful of the delicious creamy risotto.

"Yes, well," replied Morgan, as he shoveled food into his mouth, "I have to say that I am not very confident I will solve it. But I fully understand the reasons why the case has been reopened."

Elliott smiled, at least Morgan understood the reasoning behind Elliott's plan.

"You know I hold you in very high regard. I was most impressed with the way you dealt with Kelly Hudd."

Morgan forced another spoonful of food into his mouth, spilling some on his shirt, which he rubbed with a napkin, only increasing and spreading the stain that now appeared on the poorly pressed garment.

"Oh, I have news for you about that. He definitely left her, either because she was cheating, or," he paused, "get this, or because he was seeing another man."

Elliott looked puzzled. He hadn't known Tom Hudd was gay, and having two stepsons who were both homosexuals, he could usually tell.

"Come again?"

"I think," Morgan looked around him, in case anyone over heard what he was about to reveal, "I think he ran off with some guy called Doug Partridge. I think they were lovers." Morgan then explained his theory on the disappearances of Tom Hudd and Doug Partridge to Elliott. Who sat opened mouthed in disbelief at was he was hearing.

Once Morgan had finished speaking, it was Elliott's turn to talk.

"Well, that makes perfect sense," he lied. "I guess then that you are going to call off any search?"

"Absolutely, it's a total waste of time."

Elliott smiled; this was perfect. "Well, be sure to let Mrs. Hudd know. I mean, the poor girl is still looking for him. Why not let her know that you believe he had another woman, maybe even mention, in your opinion, probably as a result of her indiscretion. I wouldn't mention Doug Partridge, even though you are probably one hundred percent spot on. I think that would devastate her. Don't you agree?"

Morgan pondered for a minute, and did not reply immediately. Elliott spoke again.

"You know I have my eye on you. I see great things for you, maybe even a promotion. Who knows, you could one day lead the department, and heaven knows it needs a man like you at the helm. You would have my support."

"Really?" replied Morgan.

"Yes, of course, you are dedicated, hardworking and I like you. You do realize that I can pull strings, on your behalf, don't you?"

Morgan grinned. This was fantastic news! The Mayor liked him, and the Mayor could pull a few strings for him.

"In that case, I guess you are probably right. Maybe I will take your advice; let Mrs. Hudd know her husband is never coming back, that he found another woman, not a man. I think I could do that."

"Good," said Elliott. "You know you are my eyes and ears of the department? I think I can trust you. I *can* trust you, Jeff?"

"Absolutely," replied Morgan.

"Excellent, what do you fancy for dessert?"

Elliott Miller had a plan. The day Kelly had cried on his shoulders, hugged him and then he assisted her in the search for Tom, he had fallen in love with her. Of course, he had always found her breathtakingly attractive. In fact, Kelly Hudd was one of the most beautiful women he had ever seen. He had envied Tom Hudd, having such a gorgeous wife. Of course Elliott could only dream of one day having even the remotest chance of ever getting a crack at Kelly. Yes, it was true, she might not be bright, she may not have been what you would describe as intellectual, but many powerful men had young, beautiful wives and girlfriends. Why shouldn't he? He was powerful. He was important.

That day, the day he heard about Tom's disappearance he had been secretly pleased. Of course, like everyone else in the neighborhood, he was shocked that Tom had left his wife. Why would anyone leave Kelly Hudd? But Elliott had spotted an opportunity, an opportunity where maybe, just maybe, he could try and court Kelly Hudd.

Of course, it would be inappropriate to immediately contact her. She had eventually moved out of the neighborhood, but sooner or later he would make the call, once Morgan had delivered the bad news. He had already set the ground work, offering her his sympathy, accompanying her to the police station. He had said all the right things and felt that there was a connection now between them. He knew full well that her mental state was presently not at its best. He also knew that, by her own admission, she had no inhibitions when it came to sex. That revelation alone, her admission of adultery, had spurred Elliott. As long as Tom Hudd remained missing, and no proper search was conducted, there was a chance that maybe she would go for him.

He knew that it would take time to woo Kelly, but he could wait, and the longer Tom stayed missing, the more chances she could divorce the man in absentia, especially if she knew he had another woman. He also knew that her house was in foreclosure, and he had already made enquiries with the lending bank. He was now making her mortgage payments, and the bank had assured him that they would maintain the anonymity he had requested. Sooner or later her parents would surely tire of her moping around their home in Atlanta, sooner or later she would regain her former confidence, though of course not too much, hoped Elliott, and Elliott would be waiting for her when she returned to Savannah; her knight in shining armor….

# CHAPTER THIRTY THREE

The old man removed the Glock 19 from its box under his bed and filled the magazine with just one bullet. He then placed it on the reading table next to his easy chair, patting it gently. He then slipped outside into the late afternoon. It was dusk, the sun was setting and it was quite a pleasant evening. It was also time for someone to die, and it was time for revenge.

# CHAPTER THIRTY FOUR

Billy Malphrus needed more cigarettes. His nerves were getting the better of him. The stroll to Piggly Wiggly would do him good, he thought. He took a draw on his last cigarette and let the smoke fill his lungs. He looked skyward and wondered if his aunt was home yet. He wondered if she had drunk his lemonade, and he wondered if she was already dead. Suddenly he froze. What the hell had he been thinking? Of course there would be an autopsy. Of course he would be the prime suspect. It wouldn't take even the dumbest of detectives to put two and two together and realize that the person who had administered the poisonous lemonade to his aunt was him. It was like an epiphany. The sudden realization that he was making a huge mistake. He needed to get home, and quickly, he had to stop her drinking that damn lemonade.

He stubbed out his cigarette and looked around; if he ran he could maybe get home before she did. Suddenly another shiver ran down his spine. He hadn't noticed her, but she had been there all the time, staring at him, watching him. It was her. Gerry Gordonston, Kelly Hudd, or whatever her name was. She looked different, fatter he thought, uglier, she looked… scary. Sitting next to her in the passenger seat of her car was a dog.

Kelly stared directly at Billy Malphrus, her heart pounding. She had paid good money for him to be killed, yet here he was, alive and kicking. She had lost everything, and yet here he stood, smoking his cigarette, standing outside the Piggly Wiggly – with not a care in the world.

Billy knew the last thing he needed right now was a confrontation with the crazed looking woman parked in the car less than ten feet in front of him. Now he had two reasons to run. What if Kelly was on her way to tell Cindy everything? Before Kelly could even unfasten her seat belt, Billy dropped his cigarette and ran.

*****

Betty Jenkins pulled into the Piggly Wiggly car park with smug satisfaction, another perfect lesson, and tomorrow she would be the proud holder of a Georgia State Driving License.

"Watch out!" yelled her driving instructor. Betty instinctively applied the brakes. But it was too late, Billy Malphrus' body catapulted through the air and over her driving instructor's car. Even though Betty had applied her brakes, unfortunately for Billy, the car behind her didn't, and drove over Billy's body, which lay prone on the road, crushing his body with the front right wheel and his head with the rear right wheel.

*****

Kelly Hudd stared in disbelief at the scene unfolding before her. Then, for the first time in four months, she smiled. That morning had been tough, especially after that detective had told her that Tom had most likely run off with another woman, and that all the clues indicated that he had been the one cheating on her. The detective wouldn't say who this other woman was, but he had told her it was pointless even pursuing. She couldn't believe it; she had spent most of the day crying. But now, now she laughed. Kelly could not believe what she had just witnessed. She had stared directly at him and he had stared back. It was the first time she had seen him since Paris, apart from a few minutes earlier outside her home, and the time she had briefly glimpsed him as he arrived at Cindy's home, the night Tom had collected him from the airport, the night she had contacted those people. Those people who were meant to kill him. The 'Organization' who had taken her money and done nothing.

The look on his face when he saw Kelly had been of shock, of fear and of utter disbelief. He had dropped the cigarette he had been smoking and had seemed frozen, like an escaped prisoner, caught in a searchlight, as if tranquilized by an invisible dart.

Kelly had no plan. She wasn't even sure if she would even confront him. He had been the last person she had expected to see when she had pulled up outside her old home, and despite following him, she wasn't even sure what she was going to say to him. But then he ran, before Kelly could even think of what to do. Billy Malphrus had bolted into the road that circumnavigated the shopping area's car park, and, as if in slow motion, Kelly had seen everything. He had been hit side on, but as he hit the car entering the car park, which actually wasn't going fast at all, he had turned to face it. Kelly had sat open mouthed in her car as Billy Malphrus was tossed into the air and over the vehicle, and she had remained open mouthed as she saw the car behind enter the car park. This vehicle, however, was traveling faster than the one which had hit him.

Despite her hatred for the fraud and liar that was Billy Malprhus, she had winced as the second car ran over his head. She had nearly vomited as Billy's brains and head were crushed like a watermelon. She had put her hand to her mouth and had nearly thrown up when his brains spilled out onto the tarmac.

She sat in her car and watched as the drivers and passengers of both cars exited their vehicles and stood around the body of Billy Malphrus. She thought she recognized the black lady, the one who had been driving the car that had hit him. She had stared as onlookers and shoppers rushed to where Billy Malphrus, or whatever was left of him, lay. There was no doubt he was dead. His head was as flat as a pancake, and she could see quite clearly that there was no way Billy Malphrus could have survived such horrific injuries. As witnesses and onlookers frantically dialed 911, and a few others took photographs of Billy's corpse to no doubt tweet to their friends, Kelly smiled. For the first time in months she smiled. It was as if the depression and anxiety that had been haunting her since Tom had left her was suddenly lifted. Her smile then turned into a giggle, then her giggle into laughter, and as she sat, unnoticed by the gathering crowd, as sirens from an ambulance filled the air, her laughter grew. Her laughter grew to a crescendo, becoming hysterical, and she could not stop. And as she laughed, in the sanctuary that was her car, the crowds gathered around Billy Malphrus. People ran to see what the commotion was, not noticing the woman, sitting in her car, a confused Labrador next to her, tears of laughter streaming down her face and suddenly feeling rejuvenated, with a fresh sense of justice instilled in her, and the will to finally move on with her life.

# CHAPTER THIRTY FIVE

The old man clenched the rope he held tightly in his hand, his tattoo again appearing larger than it was, an illusion caused by the folding and puffing of the skin around it. He could see her through the window of her kitchen. He had entered her yard unheard and unnoticed, and had retrieved the rope he now carried from one of his suitcases that still sat in his living room.

* * * * *

Heidi Launer could bear it no more. She had lived a good life, but she was not prepared to have her reputation sullied and her name tarnished. Nor was she prepared to be executed without putting up a fight. She had spent the day alone in her usually locked room, alone with her memories. Before leaving her memorial to evil, she had taken her uncle's Luger, loaded the chamber and headed into her kitchen, where she now sat, Luger in hand, waiting....

* * * * *

Cindy Mopper collapsed onto her kitchen floor as the officer told her the news. Billy, poor Billy, killed less than fifteen minutes ago. Was there a neighbor they could call? A friend who could be with her. Ten minutes later Carla arrived and hugged her grieving friend.

"Billy, my Billy, he's gone," sobbed Cindy.

Carla comforted her old friend. "There, there, dear, you let it all out," she said, extremely concerned for her friend, who wasn't taking the shocking news of Billy's death at all well.

"Oh, Cindy, the officer told me what happened. I am so, so sorry. He was such a good and kind boy. He was truly one of the better ones. Let it all out, come on honey, and cry as much as you can."

Cindy clung to her friend, devastated and inconsolable. Poor Billy, his head crushed so that he was unrecognizable. His body now lay in the morgue. They had decided to remove his body as quickly as possible. It was obvious he was dead, and it was obvious what had occurred. It was, as the officer explained, a tragic accident. For some inexplicable reason he had run out in front of a car while leaving the grocery store. The poor woman who had hit him, and had in fact told the attending officers who he was, had been taking her final driving lesson.

Carla delved into her pocket and produced two bottles of pills.

"Xanax," she said, "and Ambien – I think you need to take these. Try and calm down and sleep for an hour. I will take care of Paddy. Is there anything I can get you?"

Cindy shook her head and forced a smile. Carla was indeed a good friend, and the thought of what she had once planned for her friend made her cry even harder. "No, just you being here is enough."

"Look, take these," offered Carla, handing her the medication. "I take them to take the edge off, so to speak, and they will help you sleep."

Cindy took the pills from her friend and Carla filled a glass with water from tap, which Cindy duly drank, swallowing the medication.

"Okay, you go and lie down. I will look after Paddy. I will take him for a walk, maybe come back with Walter, and they can hang out together. Leave everything to me." Carla looked around the kitchen where they stood, noticing a pile of lemons that had been recently squeezed on the kitchen counter top. "I will also tidy this place up for you. So, you just try and sleep."

Cindy kissed her friend on the cheek and made her way to bed. Carla sighed. Poor Cindy. Billy was all she had, and he seemed such a nice boy. Life, she thought, was indeed fragile. You never knew when your time was up.

Before she would do anything though, Carla needed a drink. She opened Cindy's fridge and scanned its contents and spotted a jug of yellow liquid. Ah, she thought, that explains the squeezed lemons. She removed the jug from the fridge and sniffed it. It smelled fine, a hint of mint maybe? She grabbed a glass and filled it with Billy's poisoned lemonade. Carla took a seat at the kitchen table and once again felt sorrow for not just Cindy, poor Cindy who hadn't a bad bone in her body, but of course for the unfortunate and tragic Billy, who also wouldn't harm a fly, who had spent most of his time caring for others and doing his stupendous charity work. *The good always die young,* thought Carla, as she raised the glass to her lips, but paused. First she would collect Walter, bring him to keep Paddy company, and she placed the glass back onto the table, the contents still un-drunk.

# CHAPTER THIRTY SIX

Veronica Partridge poured herself a glass of wine and relaxed on her sofa. Katie was sleeping, and this was her time to relax. She took a sip of chardonnay and smiled, stretched her legs and closed her eyes. Doug had been gone for months, and though she knew Katie missed him, it was of course for the best. At least Doug had left them financially secure. No mortgage and over $2,500,000 in the bank had meant she no longer needed to work. She had time to herself and felt like she had the chance to start all over again.

She stood from the sofa and headed to the sliding doors that led to her back yard and stared at her flower bed. Soon those flowers would cover the slight raise in the earth. It was, she thought, a nice grave, and at least he would always be near them.

She returned to the sofa, poured herself another glass of wine, and thought back to the events that had occurred a few months previously. She recalled the day vividly, the day Doug had admitted everything. His past, his actual job, the murders and the killings. He had lied to her from day one. Every word, every utterance, had been false, and from the moment he had eventually confessed all, she knew she no longer wanted him in her life. She had loved him, but how could she after his lies? Not after that; she could never trust him again.

When he had shown her the bank statement from the account that contained the money he had accumulated, she had tried to understand his motives; that he had done it for them, for Katie, for her, but she could no longer believe a word he told her. It was for the best, what had happened; the fact that he was gone, no longer with them.

*****

"I have something I have to tell you," said Doug as his wife returned to their bedroom after putting down Katie, who was now sound asleep in her room.

Veronica could tell from the tone of her husband's voice it was something serious; he sounded worried and a little nervous. His demeanor also showed his anxiousness. What was even odder was that he was dressed, especially as it was ten thirty at night. She also didn't fail to notice the small carry on suitcase that lay at the side of their bed.

Veronica felt a sudden dread overwhelm her. Was Doug leaving her? Was he about to suddenly disappear from her life, just as quickly as he had entered it? Nearly three years ago.

"Doug, what is going on?" she asked, indicating towards the suitcase.

"Sit down, Veronica, there is something I have to tell you, something I think I should have told you earlier, but I didn't have the courage. I never thought I would need to tell you, but something has happened, and I have to be honest; I have to tell you the truth about me, what I do, what I have done, and now the danger I have put myself in."

Veronica sat on the bed, as she had been instructed.

"I have to leave. Tonight. I don't have a choice. If there was any way I could stay, I would," said Doug, as he took his wife's hand.

Veronica recoiled her hand immediately. "You are leaving me? Leaving us? Why? How could you? Have you met someone else? What the hell is going on, Doug?"

"I really don't know where to start," replied Doug.

"From the beginning, how about from the beginning, Doug?" said Veronica, her arms now folded. "It usually is the best place to start."

So Doug Partridge did. He started from the beginning. He told his wife the truth. She did not interrupt as he began to explain exactly who he was and what he did.

For twenty minutes, uninterrupted and without one question from Veronica, Doug Partridge began his confession. He told her that he was not an accountant; that he never had been, that his money and investments had been earned not from toiling away in an office, not by investing in stocks and shares and not by arranging corporate mergers and acquisitions. No. He was an assassin; he killed people for money. He was a murderer, a gun for hire who had made the mistake of falling in love. Falling in love with her. He had tried to retire, tried so desperately to hide his past, to start again, to rebuild his life with Veronica and now Katie. All he had ever craved was a normal life. He was sickened by the things he had done, ashamed of them, but that was then, and this was now, and he realized that he could no longer live the lie he had been leading since the day he met Veronica and retired from the 'Organization'. For twenty minutes he pleaded his case, defending his actions where he could, and confronting his biggest fear, his wife finding out the truth.

Veronica sat open mouthed as Doug spoke. More than once she shook her head and raised her hand to her mouth. She was in shock. Her husband, the father of her child, the man she thought she knew better than any other person on the planet was a fraud and a liar, but much worse than that, he was a killer, he was a cold-blooded murderer who had killed many times.

"Look, I know this is a shock, but I needed to tell you,"

said Doug.

"A shock? A goddam shock?" screamed Veronica. "You sit there, telling me that you are a killer, a murderer, Jesus Christ; an assassin, and you say 'I know this is a shock'? How dare you, how dare you come into my life, lie to me, have a child with me and not have the courage to tell me the truth? A shock? Are you serious? This isn't you telling me you cheated, this isn't you telling me you dinged the car, this isn't you telling me that we are broke, or you have cancer. That would be a shock. This, whatever this is, is more than just a damn 'shock'!"

Doug shook his head, what had he expected? That Veronica would nod her head, say everything was fine, that 'yeah, well, it's a bit of shock, but let's just forget it'.

"Is your name even Doug?" asked Veronica, in a tone harsh and accusatory.

Doug didn't reply. He was ashamed. Ashamed of the lies he had told the only woman he had ever truly loved. Ashamed that sleeping in the room next to him was a precious child, innocent and trusting, a child that he had brought into the world, all based on the lies he had told.

"So, 'Doug,'" said Veronica aggressively, "just what the hell were you doing in Savannah when we met? I take it that was a lie, you attending that banking conference, were you here on business or on '*business*'?" Veronica was shaking, not just with anger but fear. It dawned on her that she did not know the man sitting sullen faced and remorseful in front of her. She suddenly realized that she didn't know him at all.

"I came to Savannah to kill a man," replied Doug.

"Who?" asked Veronica, fighting back tears.

"It really isn't important who he was," answered Doug as he tried to comfort his wife, who rebuked his consoling arms immediately.

"Don't you touch me!" she screamed.

Doug put his arms by his side, conscious that Katie was sleeping in the next room. The last thing he needed was for her to wake up, not right now.

"Not important? Not important?" repeated Veronica. "He would have been important to somebody," she screamed, "everyone is important; he could have been a father, a brother, he was somebody's son, maybe somebody's husband. And you say he isn't important. I despise you. I hate you. You are a vile human being, and I cannot believe I let you into my life. You are evil 'Doug'. And you are right to be ashamed. You disgust me."

Doug took a deep breath. He had not known what to expect after his confession, he had not known how Veronica would react. This though, was worse than anything he could have imagined.

"Honey, please, keep your voice down," he pleaded, indicating the room next door and their sleeping daughter.

"Honey? Don't you ever call me 'honey'."

"Veronica, I love you, I love Katie, and as soon as I met you I stopped. I retired. I thought I could start my life all over again. I gave it all up, the killing, the double life, the money, all for you."

Veronica looked at him incredulously, as if he was nothing but a piece of dirt on her shoe, a piece of dirt she wished she could scrape off.

"But you didn't tell me. You didn't tell me, you didn't love me enough to trust me. I fell in love with you, or whoever 'you' were back then. Our whole life is based on lies." She was sobbing harder now, streams of tears rolled down her face, and she put her head in her hands. "Can't you see? Can't you see what you have done? Don't you understand that everything we have done together; our life, Katie, everything, it is all a lie?"

Doug lowered his head once more in shame. What had he done? She was right of course. His whole life was a lie, and he did not know what he regretted most, the murders and the killings, the lies he had told Veronica, or the fact he had confessed.

"And for what, Doug? For what?" asked Veronica in between her tears of not only sadness but rage.

"We have nothing, we are broke, you sit at home all day while I work. I drive a crappy car. I come home and look after Katie while you write your stupid book. I read a bit of it; it is crap by the way, no one will read it anyway. You have no idea what you have done. You have destroyed this family, destroyed me. You promised me so much, you always said you were looking for work, looking for a job here in Savannah. I believed you, Doug. I believed you. And now- and now you think you can just leave, walk away? Disappear from our lives? You tell me you are in danger, that if you don't leave 'something' may happen? Just what, Doug? Just what? Are you going to be arrested, exposed for what you have done? Tell me, you son of a bitch, tell me!"

Doug did not answer immediately. He took a deep breath and reached for his briefcase and opened it.

Veronica sneered at him. "What, are you going to kill me now? Then Katie?"

Doug stared at his wife, a long cold stare that Veronica had never seen before, a stare that though it frightened her, she found attractive. Doug was a handsome man, he was fit, she found him sexy, and despite the emotions of hate and disgust she was feeling she was still attracted to him, and, though she would probably never admit it, the fact that her husband was a cold blooded killer, irrelevant of her other feelings, she still loved him.

Doug handed Veronica two pieces of paper.

"We are not broke. This money is yours, yours and Katie's. It is in an account in your name. Your name only."

Veronica took the documents. It was a bank statement in her name at a bank somewhere in the Cayman Islands, according to the letter headed pages.

Veronica put her hand to her mouth. "Oh my God," she said, "this is how much money you have?"

"Had," replied Doug "it is yours now, and Katie's, not

mine. All of it."

"I thought we were broke," said Veronica. "You told me you had retired, that you had no money, where did this come from?" she said waiving the statement in the air. "This is more money than I could ever spend. I can live off the interest alone. Doug, please, you need to tell me the truth, where did this money come from?"

For the second time that evening Doug took a deep breath.

"I came out of retirement, for the last few months I have been working again. I— "

Veronica raised her hand, indicating to Doug that she did not want to hear anymore.

"So those trips you said were job interviews, all lies?"

"Yes," answered Doug.

"So you are still killing people? You are not retired, everything you just said about retiring, about starting again, about feeling ashamed is not true? You are still killing people?"

For the first time that evening Doug lied. "No."

Veronica sighed with relief.

"The money is back pay, money I was owed; it is my severance package, so to speak," he lied again.

"It doesn't change a thing, Doug, you know that don't you?" said Veronica, as she clutched the bank statement. "You do know that things can never be the same; that it is over between us?"

Doug shook his head. "It doesn't have to be," he said. "It doesn't have to be over. Look, that money is yours, no one can take it from you, no one, it is enough for you to start a new life, enough so you never have to work again. I know I repulse you right now, but I swear, on Katie's life, there is a way we can work this out."

Veronica shook her head. "How? How on earth can we work this out?"

"I am still the man you married. What you have seen is

the real me. Yes, I had a past, yes I did some bad things, but it doesn't change the fact that I love you, that I love you with all my heart. That I love Katie. You have everything, all the money, everything, the house is even in your name. I want you to be happy, but I want you to consider something. I want you to consider that we start again. We move; we disappear and start again. I have people who will help us, help us with new identities, passports, new names. We can live anywhere. Katie will grow up happy, receive a good education and we can move on from this. I am asking for a second chance. I have been honest with you, albeit delayed, but I have told you everything."

Veronica Partridge stared at the figures on the paper in front of her. He was right. The money was enough to live on forever. Katie would be secure. But Doug? The trust was gone, he had destroyed everything. But he was still Katie's father and despite everything he was a good father.

"Then why are you leaving, Doug? Why are you in danger?" she asked.

"The people I work for," Doug corrected himself, "worked for, are finished, it is over; I don't know the full details, but it seems some people may have been compromised, some other people, I mean colleagues I guess, whom I never met obviously, and they may be on the verge of arrest. I am not sure if my name is on that list or not."

"Your name?" asked Veronica "What name? Doug, Dave, John? I don't even know your real name, do I, Doug? What list?"

Doug ignored Veronica's questions and continued to speak. "I need to leave, disappear, I have a place I can go. Until this thing settles down at least. I just need you to trust me on this. This thing is bigger than me, and I believe I am safe, but it is just too risky for me to stay here. I have to go. Your money is safe, Veronica, there is no link to me. All I am asking is that you give me a chance, help me get out of this."

"You swear to me that you are retired?" said Veronica.

"I did already. But I will again, I swear." Doug took his wife's hand, and this time she did not push him away. "I need to leave, tonight, but I promise you I want this, us, to work. I want to watch Katie grow up, I want to be with you, and I love you. If I could, I would go back in time and change everything, but I can't. Please, all I am asking for is time, and I know you need time. Just give me a second chance."

Veronica was silent. The money was in her name. The house was in her name. Doug was leaving anyway, that was obvious, his bag was packed and there was no turning back. She had options. She could simply call the police, have him arrested there and then, but if she did that… the money, would she lose it? What about Katie? Whatever decision she made, irrelevant of her feelings for Doug, had to be based on her child. The consequences of Doug being arrested could result in her losing everything; the house, the money, all of it, even if he did say it was safe. If Doug were to leave that night and not return, then she could start again on her own, just her and Katie, but Katie loved her father, and it would break her heart, but kids were resilient; she was only two, in a few years she wouldn't even remember him.

"Okay," she said finally. "I need time, a lot of time. I need to think. I need to decide what is best not just for me, but for Katie."

"I understand that," said Doug. "Look, I have it all worked out. All you need to do is tell everyone I left you, that you have no idea where I am. That I simply got up one morning and left. I have no friends here, no one even knows me, those old biddies in the park are the only ones I ever see anyway. All you need to do is report me as a missing person. That's it. You can access the money; it is totally untraceable, so think about it. You can have anything and everything you want, a new car, no need to work, spend every day with Katie. Just you and her. Give me six months, six months to let all this die down. It is all I am asking."

Veronica Partridge hated her job. She hated not being at

home with Katie. She was also envious, envious of her friends who drove nice cars, spent their afternoons shopping and their mornings working out at the gym. She was envious of those women who could get their nails done and not feel guilty about spending money, envious of those housewives who spent the day gossiping, cooking and who spent every moment they could with their children. She was envious of the soccer moms who seemed to not have a care in the world, who never seemed to struggle. She wanted more out of life. To relax, not to work, she wanted to join the Junior League, she wanted to wear nice clothes, buy jewelry, and she wanted those friends who lived those perfect lives to be envious of her. She didn't need Doug around for that, not now, she had the money.

"Veronica? Veronica?" said Doug, to his wife, who seemed to be miles away in her thoughts. "I will do anything to protect this family, anything. You and Katie are fine. Even if they are looking for me, even if I am in danger, you are not. "

"All I do is report you as missing?" asked Veronica.

"Yes, I will leave tonight, and you won't hear from me until I know it is safe. Then, if you want me back, we can start again. It is what I want. But, if you don't want me back, if you want me out of your life forever, out of Katie's life, then I will be. It is up to you."

"You know I am going to quit my job tomorrow, right?" she said. "And buy a new car?"

"You can do what you want," said Doug.

"Doug, tell me something, is this true? That we could start again? That it is over, the killings and the murders? That if I do what you ask, report you as a missing person, that Katie and I will be safe?"

Doug nodded. "Yes, I swear."

"There is no one else? This isn't just an excuse so you can run away with another woman?"

For the first time that evening Doug smiled. "No, honey, there is no 'other' woman. I have told you everything."

Veronica took a breath and sighed. She knew Doug wouldn't cheat. At least that was something. "What if I meet someone," she asked, "when you are gone? What if I fall in love and meet somebody else, then what?"

"Then I would kill him," said Doug, the cold icy stare returning to his face. "I am joking," he said, smiling. "Look, this is my mess, this is my problem, and I just hope that you wait for me. I am not going to do anything. I have to say though, I am surprised you would even think that, you know, meeting another man and all."

Veronica shook her head "Doug, I am not thinking that, it was just a question. I have no intention of meeting anyone. Anyway, the only guy I would even consider ever cheating with in this town has already left his wife and found someone else anyway, apparently."

Before Doug could respond, his wife continued, "Now I am joking. I am talking about Tom Hudd. At least you aren't leaving me for another woman like he probably did; at least you are giving me some notice."

Doug didn't respond, he simply smiled, apparently at his wife's joke.

Ten minutes later Doug left. He kissed his daughter on the forehead as she slept, clutching her stuffed rabbit as she stirred before returning to a deep sleep. He took his briefcase and the small suitcase and walked to the front door. He stared into Veronica's face.

"I do love you," he said, "and I am sorry." Veronica did not respond immediately. Despite everything, despite the fact that she didn't even know his real name, despite the fact he had lied, despite the fact she was angry, she still loved the man she had married. She still loved Doug Partridge. She still loved the Doug Partridge she had met three years ago.

"Be safe," she said as she kissed Doug on the cheek.

"I will, I promise," he replied.

"What's that?" asked Veronica, pointing to a piece of paper that she saw protruding from Doug's jacket pocket.

"Nothing, just a note from a friend."

Veronica watched as Doug disappeared into the night. She had no idea where he was heading, no idea how he would get there, or any idea when she would hear from him. She looked down at her fingers. Tomorrow she would get a manicure.

# CHAPTER THIRTY SEVEN

The cab pulled into Gordonston and he handed over a fifty dollar bill and told the driver to keep the change. He slammed the door and began to run.

* * * * *

Stefan entered her yard and could see her clearly. He tugged at the rope; it would suffice.

* * * * *

Heidi Launer knew what she really needed to do. It was either this or giving the Jew the satisfaction of either disgracing her or worse, killing her. She raised the Luger and placed it on her forehead. Heidi could feel the cold steel of the pistol against her skin. She must be brave. This was the only way. She could not live with the shame of her friends and neighbors knowing that her whole life had been a lie. Not that she wasn't proud of her history or her beliefs. She was. She was proud of her family, her uncle, the philosophy that he had preached. As far as she was concerned, it was nothing to be ashamed of. But others, others would not understand, they would banish her from the community, she would be shunned, no one would speak to her, these pathetic Americans with the false ideals and ridiculous notions. No, she would rather die a noble death than become an outcast. Let them find out the truth after her death. Let them say what they wanted. As long as she was not around to hear it, what did she care?

Heidi drew in a deep breath and sat upright in her chair. She rose. With the Luger in her right hand, now firmly pressed against her forehead, she lifted her left hand skyward, and, just before she pressed the trigger, at the top of her voice, shouted, "Siege Heil!"

# CHAPTER THIRTY EIGHT

Carla returned to Cindy's home and let herself in. Walter immediately rushed to play with his old friend Paddy. Cindy was still sleeping, and Carla also felt tired. She sat back on the chair by the kitchen table and sighed. Death. So unpredictable, like life really. How ironic; a nice boy like Billy being killed so young, while others went through life hurting, lying and cheating, and not a bad thing ever happened to them. But sometimes, sometimes people did get their comeuppance....

* * * * *

She had noticed him the moment he and Kelly had arrived in Gordonston. He was simply a beautiful looking man; rugged and handsome, fit, charming and he just oozed sex appeal. Carla, by her own admittance, had had many lovers. She knew that she looked half her age, she knew she was still an attractive woman, but even she could not surely compete with the looks of Kelly Hudd.

Carla Zipp had, for the most part, always gotten what she wanted. As a dancer in Las Vegas she had many men at her fingertips who would fawn over her, wine and dine her, buy her expensive gifts, jewelry and clothes. She was never short of admirers. She had become used to the attention and half expected it. Gino, especially, had declared his undying love for her, and of course it had been he to whom she had turned whenever she needed anything. No matter where she went, she was always the woman other women envied and their husbands desired.

The only thing Carla hadn't got, something that she truly wanted, was a happy marriage. Her husband, Ian, had it all, a great job, money and a wife over whom his friends and colleagues lusted. But that hadn't been enough for him. More than anything, Ian's cheating with his younger secretary had hurt Carla's pride. Mainly because Carla considered herself more attractive than the floozy who was sleeping with her boss, Carla's husband. It was, of course, her old flame Gino who had restored her pride. She had played the role of grieving and betrayed widow perfectly. For many of her husband's former friends it was inconceivable he would even consider cheating on his wife. But he had and he had paid the price for it.

Carla Zipp felt that she deserved a man who was compatible with her looks and sex appeal, and only one man she knew fit that bill – Tom Hudd. She had desired him from afar, just as others had desired her. She was jealous of Kelly – how lucky that girl was to have a husband like Tom. Carla felt that it was as if Kelly was a younger version of her, but living the perfect life that had eluded Carla. Whenever Kelly would appear at the park with Shmitty, she would force a smile and join in with compliments with Heidi and Cindy about how beautiful Kelly was, how she had the perfect life, how she should really be a model. But behind the false smile and behind the compliments Carla had a plan. She would get what she wanted one day. She would get Tom Hudd.

* * * * *

Carla opened her eyes, and reached for the glass of lemonade on Cindy's table. She raised it to her lips, but before she could drink, Walter and Paddy came rushing into the kitchen. "Calm down you two," she scolded, "you will wake poor Cindy."

She closed her eyes again and recalled the day she and Tom had met in the park, the day that she had once again gotten what she had wanted, the day that would eventually lead to the death of Tom.

* * * * *

The Gordonston Ladies Dog Walking Club had adjourned their afternoon session in the park. Cocktails had been drunk, dogs had been exercised and gossip had been shared. Heidi and Cindy had retrieved Fuchsl and Paddy, but Walter was not cooperating. He was too interested in a squirrel he had been chasing that had climbed a tree. Walter was ignoring his mistress' commands to heel. As far as he was concerned, this pesky squirrel was far more important than going home to be fed.

"You two go on without me," she had told Cindy and Heidi. "Walter is playing one of his silly squirrel games. I will see you both tomorrow." Her friends made their farewells and Carla headed toward where Walter sat, under a tree, his tail wagging, waiting for his new playmate to resume their game.

Tom had arrived in the park just minutes after Cindy and Heidi had left. Carla spotted him immediately and a sudden feeling of excitement engulfed her. Her heartbeat quickened and a surge of adrenalin seemed to ooze through her body. This was the first time she had ever seen him alone, without his wife at his side, and she without either Heidi or Cindy. Was this fate? Had this been preordained? She had dreamt of this moment, lived it in her dreams, fantasied about her and Tom alone, and now she would at last have the chance to at least speak to the man of her dreams. Maybe this would be the opportunity she needed; the opportunity she needed to bed Tom Hudd. Being prepared for anything was one of Carla's strengths, and she supposed one of her mottos. The expensive boob job she'd had was for him, so he would notice her. The clothes which she wore, that she knew had incurred the disdain of Cindy and Heidi, were designed to be sexy, to attract, to snare. She wore tight figure hugging jeans, a tight leather jacket so her new breasts could not be ignored. Her hair and make-up were always perfect. Every day she had dressed like this since she had decided enough was enough, that if she was going to have any chance of ever getting Tom Hudd to notice her then everything and anything could help. And here he was, walking his dog alone in the park. And here she was, a predator ready to pounce, her claws already sharpened.

"Hi," said Tom as he approached Carla, unleashing Shmitty, who headed towards Walter, apparently curious as to why the bulldog was staring at a tree.

Carla took a deep breath; she would play it cool, this wasn't going to be easy she was sure, but if it was ever going to happen, this was the perfect opportunity to start the ball rolling.

"Why hello," she replied as Tom neared. "I hardly ever see you in the park. It's usually your wife who takes out the dog, isn't it?"

"Usually, yes, but she has kind of abandoned me. She is in Europe, France, Paris to be exact, having fun no doubt, so I am on dog duty," he replied, pointing towards Shmitty, who was now chasing Walter in a playful game. "You are Carla, aren't you? My wife talks about you all the time, says that you are a regular customer of hers. Probably one of her best."

That was probably true. Carla often visited Macy's and Kelly's beauty counter. In fact, just lately she had spent well over $500 on products, especially anti-aging creams and foundation, all of course, for the sole purpose of attracting a man. Not just any man. But the man who stood right there in front of her.

"Oh, that's nice to hear," said Carla. It wasn't. It wasn't nice to hear at all. Did that mean that Kelly Hudd was mocking her? Discussing how much she spent on beauty products? That bitch, that nasty little bitch, well, if that was the case she would shop elsewhere. Was she seen as a joke in the Hudd household? She pushed the thought from her mind. Stay on point, she told herself, stay focused.

"She says you are wasting time though," smiled Tom. "You don't need anything, she tells me. Honestly, you are her role model. She constantly tells me that 'when I get to be forty I hope look like Carla Zipp; the woman is just beautiful', she says it all the time. You have a big fan there."

Carla's heart almost missed a beat. Kelly Hudd envied her? Kelly Hudd thought she was only forty? She was Kelly's role model? Best of all though, that meant Tom only thought she was forty. This might be easier than she had initially anticipated.

"I have to agree with her," said Tom, flashing a pearly white smile. "I sure hope Kelly looks like you when she turns forty; I wouldn't be able to keep my hands off her. How do you do it? You look great?"

And that was all Carla needed to hear. That was her cue. She knew Tom Hudd, despite his beautiful wife, despite his reputation as being a good hard working man, despite being the 'saint' of the neighborhood, was like every other man she had ever met. He did not think with his brain. He was human. It was time to go to work.

"Why, thank you, Tom," smiled Carla, as she discreetly pushed out her chest. "That is so nice of you to say. I am sure that if I was Kelly when she reaches my age, forty, that I wouldn't object to having your hands all over me."

Tom and Carla both laughed at Carla's comment. For a moment, Carla thought that he even blushed.

"Now, tell me, why have you been abandoned? I know if you were my husband I would not let you out of my sight."

Tom nodded and smiled, he stroked his thick black hair with his hand, and this time Carla was sure that he was blushing. Carla had no idea what he was thinking, but she could guess; she had a sixth sense when it came to men. Midafternoon, bored no doubt, obviously thinking about sex; she had read somewhere that men think about sex eight thousand times a day. If that was true she did not know, but she had also read, again God only knew where, that every time a man encounters a woman, he weighs her up as a potential sexual partner, and she knew that was exactly what Tom was doing that minute.

Tom grinned. That was a good sign, thought Carla. He was obviously flattered by her last comment.

"Well, I asked her not to go without me, but she insisted. I only hope that she is okay; she hasn't called yet. You know, it is kind of hard being on my own. I have taken time off from work, you know, to look after the dog, that sort of thing, and I guess I am a little bored. Haven't eaten anything decent for days, just takeout food and the odd sandwich."

"Well, it doesn't seem to be doing you any harm," said Carla, who made a point of looking Tom up and down, obviously admiring his physique, and making sure Tom knew it.

They were flirting and Carla was enjoying it and she could tell Tom was also. It was time to make her move.

"I tell you what," said Carla, "and I hope you don't take this wrong way, but why don't I cook you something nice and healthy to eat. You know, so you can maintain that perfect body of yours."

Tom stared at Carla, and it was now obvious what was going through his mind. Carla knew he wanted her; he was bored, and he had not had sex for at least three days, as Carla knew Kelly had left Savannah three days earlier. She had him, she was sure. It all depended on his response.

"Well," said Tom, rubbing his chin, "I wouldn't want to put you to any trouble, but I do have a very well stocked pantry. I wouldn't say no to a tasty dish right now."

The flirting had just gone up a notch. There was now no doubt in Carla's mind she would be spending the afternoon in the arms of Tom Hudd. She knew men, and he had practically invited her to his home to cook. Cooking, though, is not what either of them had in mind. Though it did rhyme with it.

"I am sure your pantry is very well stocked," said Carla with a smile, "and I think I know what tasty dish would really whet your appetite."

Tom folded his muscular arms and put a foot on a felled tree stump. "Really? Something I could get my teeth into? Maybe you fancy a nibble just as much as I do?"

"Maybe I do," said Carla, "maybe I do."

"Tell you what, why don't you come over now," said Tom. "I am practically starving. I really need to deal with this enormous appetite I have."

"Well," said Carla, "I could certainly use something inside me right me now."

Thirty minutes later Tom Hudd and Carla Zipp were satisfying their appetites, and not an ounce of food had been consumed. Carla had snared her man, and it had been easier than she had thought. Sadly though, the sex hadn't been as good as she had imagined.

Tom, for all his good looks and charm, was a selfish lover. Carla was used to men who worshiped her body, who made love to her passionately. Tom Hudd was not as enthusiastic as she had hoped he would be. For him it was just sex. A relief from the boredom he felt, a chance to get laid, and deep down Carla knew it. Yes, she had enjoyed it, yes she was extremely aroused by Tom, but there was something missing. She wasn't used to being used, she was the user, but once satisfied, it was apparent to her that this time she was the one being used. Then of course came the phone call.

Kelly calling from Paris. Tom brushing away Carla's accidental cough as being the dog. Despite this, though, she still wanted him. Maybe she could change him, mold him into the lover she yearned for. She had gone this far - why stop now?

"Now," said Tom, after he had ended his call with Kelly,

"what about those casseroles you promised me?"

Carla had returned home disappointed. She had cooked Tom two casseroles and helped him clean his house. They had even gone to the store together to buy cleaning supplies. Thank God they hadn't been spotted by any of the neighbors, she thought. Carla, though, still wanted more. She still wanted Tom Hudd. Call it desire, call it lust, and call it a need to be associated with a man who complimented her looks; to satisfy her own need to be desired by someone she desired.

The truth was that Tom Hudd had no intention of seeing Carla again. He had no intention of ever leaving his wife. He had used her, used her as she had used hundreds of men in the past. It was sex. Nothing more and nothing less.

And then Kelly returned home. It was Cindy who had told Carla the truth, that Tom had no passport, that the story he had told Carla had been nothing more than lies. She sat and listened, a false smile masking her despair and anger, as Cindy explained to both Carla and Heidi how Tom had not only cleaned the house from top to bottom, but also made a delicious casserole for his wife as a surprise.

Carla had been furious, and now, four months later, felt no regret for the death of Tom Hudd. He had deserved it. There was no way she was ever going to become the butt of jokes, told to his friends at the fire station, and there was no way she was ever going to be able to bear to look at Tom, let alone at him and Kelly together. In her eyes, she had done Kelly a favor; she deserved better. If anything, Carla had stopped Kelly from spending her life with a no good cheating dog. And Carla should know, she had once been married to a man just like Tom. She had saved Kelly from a life of heartache. If anything, if Kelly actually knew the truth, she should thank Carla.

* * * * *

Putting thoughts of Tom Hudd out her mind, Carla reached for the glass of lemonade; she was parched. She raised the glass to her lips, and drank.

* * * * *

Cindy Mopper, despite the pills Carla had given to her, could not sleep, and she was sure she had just heard two loud bangs. She got out of bed and headed downstairs hoping that Carla was still there, or maybe had even gone to fetch Walter to play with Paddy.

# CHAPTER THIRTY NINE

Veronica Partridge decided she would have a bath and an early night. She was tired. She still hadn't recovered from all the digging and the burial of poor Bern, the Partridge family's loyal German shepherd who had died peacefully at the vet's office the week before. It had been a tough evening, not only digging the grave herself, but trying to bury the poor dog without Katie seeing. Katie, she knew, would have been devastated to discover her dog had died. At least she had followed all of Doug's instructions to the letter. He had told her how deep to dig the grave, and of course he had a supply of lime salts in the shed. Doug was good at leaving instructions, and though she had no respect for his chosen profession and had insisted he leave, she had done what he had asked. Reported him as a missing person, for one thing, a month after he left, as well as reconsider her divorce request. Maybe she would. Maybe she would give him a second chance. After all, at least he was a good father, and when he had called her, the same day Bern had died, he had sounded so sad when she had told him the news. Maybe he wasn't a monster after all. She raised her glass of wine to her lips and took a sip, before falling asleep on the sofa.

* * * * *

Stefan Derepaska had never gotten over the murder of his son, and never would. Killed by an assassin's bullet. Murdered because he simply knew too much about the financial dealings of the man he worked for. He had left a wife and two children. Stefan Derepaska had spent years tracing and hunting down those responsible for the murder of his only child. He had taken on many identities, many guises, and meticulously searched and eventually killed all those responsible for his son's death, including the man who had paid for and ordered his son's murder. Only one person remained, the man who had pulled the trigger. And if he couldn't find him, then he would find and kill the one closest to him. Stefan Derepaska opened the sliding door that led from Veronica Partridges' yard to her den and approached the snoozing woman, where she lay on the couch, an empty glass of wine sat on the floor. He placed the rope around her neck and squeezed tightly. Veronica awoke, confused as to what was occurring. She struggled violently, trying to force the old man to loosen his grip. She had never seen him before, had no idea who he was. What she did know, in those final seconds of her life, was that he was choking her, strangling her. She coughed, spluttered, and eventually her grip on the old man's arm loosened, her hand flopping to her side. Derepaska removed the rope from her neck, and placed a finger on her neck, checking for a pulse. It was done. An eye for an eye, a tooth for a tooth.

* * * * *

Doug Partridge kicked open the front door of his former home; the cab he had taken from the airport had gotten stuck in traffic along Bay Street. He had urged the driver to speed up, to take a quicker route, but it was late afternoon and early evening, and all the roads leading eastward were snarled with commuters eager to get home. The house was silent. He called out Veronica's name, but there was no reply. He headed to the den, positive he had heard the sliding door that led to the backyard opening.

* * * * *

Cindy Mopper felt drowsy; a result of the medication given to her by Carla. As she made her way downstairs, for a fleeting moment, she felt fine. Then the realization dawned on her and she remembered. Billy was dead. Kind-hearted, charitable and loving Billy was gone. She closed her eyes as a wave of grief overcame her and tears filled her eyes. She clung to the bannister for support, as once again she felt faint.

The poor boy. The police officer who had broken the news to her had told Cindy that Billy had been hit by two cars. The first car had catapulted him into the air, while the second car, following the first one, at speed, had crushed his head. She had nearly fainted when given the news. The officer had been kind, and he had offered to sit with her until a friend could be with her. She had, of course, asked to see Billy's body, but the officer had been blunt and straight to the point, she wouldn't even recognize him, so bad were the injuries he had sustained.

Of course she had called her best friend, Carla Zipp, who had arrived within minutes. Cindy felt a pang of guilt. How could she have ever wanted to do her friend any harm? How could she have plotted Carla's death? And for what? Out of a misguided jealousy that was so misplaced and utterly ridiculous. Cindy could not believe she had even contemplated such a thing. Murder; it was abhorrent to her. Cindy cried even more and her stomach knotted. Billy was gone. He was the only person about whom she cared and who had really cared for her.

It was three hours ago that Carla had arrived and given her Xanax and Ambien and told her to sleep. The medications had a bad effect on her though, and she wondered, briefly, why Carla even took them. Still groggy, she continued her descent.

As Cindy reached the first floor of her home and entered

the hallway that led into her kitchen, she shouted for Carla. There was no reply. Maybe she had left, maybe she had taken the dogs out for a walk, probably to the park. No. She heard barking, Paddy, and then Walter, both barking, responding to her voice.

"Shush, you two," she said as she put her hand to her forehead. She really didn't need barking pooches right now. As well as the grogginess, she felt pain in her head. But why were they barking so manically? What was wrong with them? Paddy never created a commotion like this, and she was sure Walter wasn't the type of dog who barked for no reason. Her head pounded, the thumping pain in her right side lobe increasing. She must be dehydrated, she thought, she needed a drink. Suddenly another wave of grief engulfed her. Billy's lemonade. The lemonade he had made for her. The kind, oh so dear boy, always thinking about others, never himself. She was parched, and the first thing she would do would be to drink Billy's lemonade. Poor Billy, now lying on a mortuary slab with his head crushed and his body lifeless.

As Cindy entered her kitchen, both Walter and Paddy ran towards her, continuing their incessant barking.

Then she saw Carla.

She was lying prone on the kitchen floor. Walter ran to his mistress and began to whine, as if trying to guide Cindy towards her. He stared at Cindy, as if pleading with her to do something, as he turned his head to his mistress and then back to Cindy.

"Oh my God," said Cindy, putting her hand to her mouth. "Carla! Carla!" she screamed as she rushed to where her friend lay. "Carla, wake up," she said as she shook her friend, in a futile attempt to wake her. Cindy turned Carla's body to face her and froze in horror. Carla's eyes were open, fixed as if staring at some invincible horror. Cindy put her hand to her mouth, then screamed. "Carla, wake up, please, wake up!" But Carla didn't respond. Cindy had no idea how long Carla had lain on the kitchen floor. She shook her again, but still her friend did not respond.

Cindy burst into tears for the umpteenth time that day, uncontrollable tears of grief, shock and fear. She shook as she cradled her friend in her arms. Cindy did not care or seem to notice that as she cradled her dead friend in her arms, she did so sitting in a pool of vomit. She did not care as she gently stroked her friend's hair that it was matted with more vomit. She looked around the kitchen, confused as to what had caused her friend's demise. Both Walter and Paddy were now whining; the sound, mixed with Cindy's sobbing, filling the home with a macabre, even haunting noise. Cindy looked up, her heart broken twice in one day, sitting on her kitchen table was Billy's pitcher of lemonade and a glass, half full.

"Help!" shouted Cindy. "Somebody please help!"

* * * * *

Doug Partridge rushed into the den, stumbling as he tripped over the step that stood at the entrance between the kitchen and the room where his wife lay. He breathed a sigh of relief. She was sleeping soundly on the sofa.

"Veronica," he said as he walked towards her.

As he approached his wife from the rear and then stood in front of where she lay, he put his hand to his mouth. She was dead. Her eyes open and fixed in terror. Doug Partridge stepped backwards. As he did, he stepped on the shattered glass on the floor, the remnants of his wife's wine glass. He touched his wife's face. She was still warm. Whoever had done this was close. He looked at the screen door. It was partially ajar. He rushed over and pulled it fully open and entered the back yard, but he saw no one. His eyes momentarily glanced at the mound of earth that filled his wife's flower bed. Bern's grave, which his wife had dug a few weeks earlier. Suddenly he heard a noise, coming from deeper inside the house.

Katie. Oh my God, he thought, Katie.

Doug ran back into the house and rushed into his daughter's bedroom. Katie opened her eyes and smiled,

"Daddy – you're home."

# CHAPTER FORTY

Stefan Derepaska sat in his easy chair. He had done what he had needed to do. Obtained the revenge he had craved. They had all been punished. He stood and walked over to his mantelpiece and retrieved a photograph of his son. He kissed it.

"For you, Vladimir; you can rest in peace at last." He then returned to the mantelpiece, collected all his photographs, the pictures of his parents, his grandchildren, his dead wife and placed them around the easy chair, he then collected every other photograph he had brought with him from Kiev, and did the same. He returned to the easy chair and sat. He stared at the faces on the images laid out in front of him, his family, his loved ones, all innocents.

He reached for the Glock 19, which sat, with one bullet in its chamber, on the table next to his chair. He placed the gun against his forehead. He had one final regret. He had found the woman in the park extremely attractive. Heidi, that had been her name, had reminded him of his dead wife. Maybe, if things had been different, he would have asked her out for dinner, maybe they could have become friends. He shrugged, pushed the gun harder against his left temple and pulled the trigger.

*****

Doug Partridge clutched the letter he had received a month previously; the envelope had been postmarked as being mailed from Savannah. The note had been to the point and brief. The sender had been Ignatius Jackson, the old black man who he had seen often walking his dog in the park. The old man who lived in the house by the park, the large house with the turret. It had simply said, "You and your family are in danger. I know who you are. Leave Savannah, then come back and get your family. Someone is coming. Ignatius Jackson, your Director."

He had told Katie to wait in her room, told her that they were going on a trip, and he was now busy packing a bag for her. She had asked him if mommy would be going too, on their adventure. He had told her yes, but later, mommy was sleeping and would join them soon. Katie needed to be quiet, so as not to wake her. The last thing he wanted was for Katie to see her mother's body. They had to leave, and they had to leave now. Whoever had killed Veronica was close. Doug Partridge's only priority now was to protect his child.

# CHAPTER FORTY ONE

"Jesus Christ, what happened here?' said Police Chief Sam Taylor as he exited his unmarked police vehicle. The scene was simply unbelievable. It was as if every police officer and squad car available to the Savannah Police Department had descended on Gordonston. The quaint and usually quiet neighborhood streets were swarming with police officers, TV news crews, fire fighters and medical first responders.

"It's like a bomb has gone off or something. Can someone please explain to me what is happening?" he yelled again, and this time a Sergeant finally answered him.

"Sir, well, I am not sure where to begin. Last night we had reports of shots being fired in this vicinity, two to be exact. However, they weren't shots, it was some old car backfiring. Anyway, we investigated and found nothing. This morning, Detective Morgan arrived at a house on Kinzie Avenue. He had some questions for the occupant, a Mrs. Veronica Partridge. Well, it seems the door had been forced open, so he entered. He found her dead on her sofa. It looks as if she had been strangled."

Chief Taylor scratched his head.

"Anyway, the forensic guys are in there now." The officer flipped open his notebook. "She had recently reported her husband, Doug Partridge, as a missing person. The thing is, it isn't just a homicide; she had a two year old child and she is missing. As soon as we get some prints I will update you."

Taylor shook his head. "Oh my God — and what the hell happened on Henry Street? What is going on over there?"

"Someone reported hearing a shot, and initially it was suspected it was another car backfiring. After Morgan discovered the victim in the house on Kinzie, we sent some guys over to the vicinity, Henry Street. They found a house with its door ajar and proceeded to enter. We are trying to identify the victim." The Sergeant swallowed. "Looks like a suicide; self-inflicted gunshot wound to the forehead. Apparently there is nothing identifying him. Old guy. Morgan is over there now. Apparently the crime scene guys didn't want him hanging around the other murder scene. You know, he is a bit of a klutz, so they told him to leave."

Chief Taylor once again shook his head then scratched it. That was probably a good idea. The last thing they needed was Jeff Morgan contaminating another crime scene.

"Other murder scene?" asked Taylor. "You mean there is more?" Suddenly picking up on the Sergeant's previous comments.

"Yes, this morning at around eight am we received a 911 call from a Cindy Mopper. Said she found her friend dead on her kitchen floor. The victim is a woman by the name of Zipp. Carla Zipp. This one is even stranger. She, Mopper, claims she found her last night, Zipp that is, but she, Mopper, said she couldn't bring herself to call us. No solid explanation as to why. Claims she collapsed in shock, woke up this morning and called us and reported her friend dead. The Mopper woman is claiming she had taken a sleeping pill and a Xanax, so that's why she didn't call sooner. Said she was disorientated. Anyway, it looks like a clear case of poison. The tech guys found a computer with multiple internet search histories on it — poison, hit men — looks like this had been planned for a while. They are questioning her now at the station."

"This is unbelievable. Anything else, Sergeant Fuller?"

The veteran Sergeant shook his head. "Funny, I know this area. My old high school teacher lives here, had to once tell him that his wife had died in a car accident. You may remember the case, that TJ Robertson debacle. Remember him, disappeared a few months after the accident?"

Taylor nodded, indicating that he did indeed recall TJ Robertson, a nasty piece of work. He had not shed any tears when he had heard he had vanished.

Taylor reviewed the scene around him. The once quiet neighborhood of Gordonston was swarming with activity.

"Okay — this is a mess, so let me get this straight, two murders, one suicide, one missing child, anything else?" he asked Sergeant Fuller.

"Just one more thing. A woman was found sitting in her car laughing hysterically. She has been sent to Memorial hospital. She is under observation. She is incoherent, babbling about justice and then falling into fits of giggles. She isn't a suspect, but funnily enough did witness a horrific car accident yesterday involving her neighbor, who, coincidentally is, I mean was, Mopper's nephew."

"Remind me who Mopper is again?"

"The woman who poisoned her friend. Apparently."

Taylor once again shook his head. "Call Morgan, tell him I am on my way to Henry Street, to the suicide scene."

# CHAPTER FORTY TWO

Jeff Morgan hated suicides. Really, what was there to investigate? Why couldn't he be the one investigating the murder of Veronica Partridge. He had been the one who had found her after all? Maybe that's why the Chief was on his way over right now. To put his best man on the job.

"Well," said the Chief as he entered Derepaska's home, "who is he?"

"Not sure," replied Morgan. "No driving license, nothing, can't even find a passport. Apparently he only just moved in, according to the neighbor. Anyway, we are waiting for someone to get back to us regarding whose name is on the deeds. Seems he is renting this place, so maybe the owner knows who he is. Not a scrap of paper identifying him. Just three empty suitcases, some boxes and a few old photos. And of course the gun."

Morgan indicated a pile of photographs. "Looks like they were taken abroad. I haven't looked at them all yet, but none of these places seem to be in America." He began sifting through the framed images and continued to speak. "You know the victim on Kinzie? I saw her this week; she was reporting her husband as missing, which was odd, as he had been missing for a month, and it took her over three weeks to make the report. Maybe you want me over there. Maybe he did it, the husband? Came back and killed her and took the kid. You know, so he and his boyfriend could live as a family."

Taylor look puzzled. "What on earth are you talking about?" he asked Morgan.

Morgan, while still examining the photographs, explained to his Chief about the two missing person's cases he had 'successfully' solved. How it was obvious that Tom Hudd and Doug Partridge had been secret lovers and had ran away together. His new theory now included murder. Maybe Partridge had returned, killed his wife and kidnapped his daughter.

"You are kidding me?" said Chief Taylor. "That is your theory. Have you not seen what is happening here? How many coincidences does it take? Look, get that Glock over to ballistics - and stop looking at those damn photographs. And no, I don't want you going over to the murder scene on Kinzie. I want you here, so keep searching. There must be something that can identify him in this house.

Morgan did not reply. In fact, he did not even hear his superior's voice, nor listen to his instructions. He was too busy staring in disbelief at the framed photograph he now held in his hand.

"What is it?" asked Taylor, noticing his detective's sudden silence.

Morgan rose from where he knelt and handed Taylor the photograph that had left him speechless.

"Oh my God," said Taylor, "is that who I think it is?"

Morgan nodded. "Yep, it's this guy," he said pointing to the corpse with the left side of his head blown off, "and Vladimir Derepaska. I should know, I spent yesterday meticulously going through the file. I could recognize him anywhere."

# CHAPTER FORTY THREE

Elliott Miller sat at the picnic table that was usually the domain of The Gordonston Ladies Dog Walking Club. He looked disheveled, tired and worried. Chief Taylor sat opposite him.

"Some neighborhood you have here," said Taylor. Elliott didn't speak, just shook his head. "Well, I do have some good news," continued the Chief of police, "a lead on the Derepaska case. Looks like we may have a connection. The old fellow who blew his brains out could be his father. Looks like he was here looking for revenge. The weapon he used to shoot himself is with ballistics. We also found a rope; the forensics boys have it. I am not a gambling man, but I have feeling it is going to contain DNA traces that match Veronica Partridge. We also took his prints and sent them to the FBI and Interpol. I am pretty sure we are going to find matching prints all over Veronica Partridge's house. Which of course leaves us still with more questions than answers."

Elliott sighed heavily. What the hell was happening? How could this be? Gordonston was a quiet, almost perfect neighborhood. Two murders, a suicide? All in the same night? "Any sign of the child? Or possibly even Doug Partridge?" asked Elliott.

Taylor shook his head. "And that's where things get even more interesting. We ran his name through the FBI computer – nothing came back. And I mean nothing. The man is a ghost, doesn't exist. Next thing you know I get a call from the Feds, asked me why I had even entered his name into the computer. I mean, Elliott, not just the Feds, but the CIA were on my case. Told me he is linked to something big. Bigger than all of this. I am not sure how, but this is bigger than Savannah, definitely bigger than Gordonston. I am not sure what the hell is going on, but I have feeling that maybe some of this is linked. Look over there."

Elliott looked towards where the Chief was pointing. Three black vans had appeared along Edgewood Road. Six men wearing dark suits and sunglasses, with communication pieces attached to their ears, stood by the vans, apparently waiting for instructions.

"Something about National Security, and they have already flashed badges and credentials at my boys. They have told Morgan to leave Derepaska's house; confiscated everything. Sealed the place off. Looks like they are waiting to swarm over to Kinzie. Wouldn't surprise me if they did the same there. The Georgia Bureau of Investigation is also on their way over."

"And Cindy Mopper?" asked Elliott, the concern in his voice apparent. "I know the woman; I have known her for years. She wouldn't hurt a fly. For God's sake, her nephew was killed yesterday in a traffic accident. It just doesn't make sense. It's like something from an over complicated novel. It is madness. She and Carla Zipp were firm friends; there is no way I can believe she killed her. It just doesn't add up. "

Taylor didn't respond immediately but stared off into the park.

"Those your dogs?"

Elliott didn't looked up. "Yes. Biscuits and Grits. They were my late wife's poodles, my poodles now."

"And the others. The other dogs?" asked Taylor.

Elliott looked up and followed Taylor's gaze towards the far corner of the park. Biscuit and Grits had been joined by Paddy and Walter and what appeared to be a white Cairn terrier. All three dogs seemed to be digging frantically.

"Oh no. I forgot about the dogs. Cindy and Carla had dogs. They must have gotten out of her house, or she let them out. They had this little club, my wife's idea originally. They called themselves The Gordonston Ladies Dog Walking Club, and there were three of them, Cindy, Carla, and my next door neighbor Heidi. I am actually surprised she isn't out here; she is a bit of a nosy old crone; completely harmless, but loves to gossip. They all did. I guess we need to get them and call the pound. Poor dogs. That little white one, I believe he belongs to the old guy who lives in the house with the turret. He must have slipped through the railings and gotten out.

Elliott and Chief Taylor stood up from the picnic table and headed towards the dogs. Elliott had Biscuit and Grits' leashes with him. They could tie them to the picnic table before they called the pound.

As they approached the dogs, both men saw that they had indeed been digging. Each dog stood with its tail wagging, each with a bone in its mouth, as if boasting to each other who had the biggest.

"What the hell is that?" exclaimed Chief Taylor as he approached Paddy. The Irish terrier had a large bone in his mouth. He tried to grab it from Paddy, but a game of tug war ensued, between man and beast, the dog refusing to give up his recent find.

"Let go of it, there's a good boy," cajoled the police Chief, trying to negotiate with the animal. "Jesus Christ," shouted Elliott, causing Chief Taylor to loosen his grip on the bone he had been fighting Paddy for, resulting in Paddy speeding away to find a secluded corner where he could chew.

"Look down there. It's a skull; there is a body down there! They are playing with human bones!" shouted Elliott.

Elliott covered his mouth, not just in shock, but because he thought he was about to vomit. Chief Taylor reached for his radio, not before wiping his hands on his uniform.

"I need all available officers to the park immediately. Now," he screamed.

Chalky, Ignatius Jackson's Cairn terrier was the second dog to bolt. With a bone the size of a human shin bone in his mouth, with remnants of lime green cloth attached to it, he ran towards the wrought iron fence that separated the park from his home.

Just as Chalky bolted with Tom Hudd's shin bone his prize, firmly gripped in his mouth, Detective Jeff Morgan entered the park.

"Catch that dog," screamed Taylor to Morgan. "I think we just found Tom Hudd!"

Morgan, initially confused, and wondering why his boss was playing fetch with a group of dogs, especially on a morning like this, sprang into action. With his weight and general fitness impeding his chances of reaching Chalky, he still gave chase, but he was seconds too late to stop Chalky shimming through the iron railings and entering his back yard before running through the open door of his home.

Morgan turned towards his boss and shrugged. Panting and out of breath, he bent over and placed his hands on his knees.

"Climb over the fence, you moron!" shouted Chief Taylor, who was preoccupied with cornering Walter, who appeared to have another bone belonging to Tom Hudd in his mouth.

Morgan shrugged, and stared at the posts separating the park from Ignatius Jackson's back yard. Climbing over the railings, he thought, was going to be easier said than done. He placed his chubby hands on two spiked railings and heaved his hefty body upwards; he only rose an inch. He tried again, and this time he managed to scale the barrier, but only after tearing his trousers. Chalky was in the yard, gnawing on the bone. As soon as he spotted Morgan, he turned, bone in mouth, and ran through the empty door into his home.

Morgan gave chase again, his torn slacks revealing that he wore blue underpants. As he entered the home of Ignatius Jackson the smell immediately hit him. He wretched, and then vomited all over Ignatius's kitchen floor. He delved into his pocket and produced a handkerchief, which he used to cover his mouth. He caught a glimpse of Chalky as he disappeared up the stairs, and the detective followed, trying desperately not to vomit again as the smell of rotting and decaying flesh grew stronger.

He found Chalky sat beside Ignatius' bed.

"Oh for God's sake," said Morgan as he stared at the decomposing corpse of Ignatius Jackson, which had become matted and attached to the bed where his body lay. "Here boy, that's a good dog. Give me that bone," said Morgan as he edged towards Chalky. Chalky, though, was not about to give up his prize without a struggle and once again bolted, this time into Ignatius's office.

Morgan once again gave chase and followed the tiny dog as he entered the office. Chalky, now bored with the game, dropped the bone and sauntered back to guard the body of his dead master. Morgan shrugged as he bent down to pick up Tom Hudd's left shin bone and held it in front of his face. A lime green remnant of a pair of jogging pants, covered in Chalky's saliva, dangled precariously from the first part of Tom Hudd's skeleton, now in the ungloved hands of the detective.

As he rose, he glanced at the desk that sat facing the window that overlooked the park. On it was a file, marked "Gordonston". Morgan placed the bone on the desk and opened the file. Inside were photographs and a set of notes, four to be exact. He recognized them all. Tom Hudd, Billy Malphrus, Carla Zipp, and finally Elliott Miller. What the hell was this? He thought, *the Chief really needs to see these*. As he turned to leave the office, he noticed two more things lying on the office floor, and he bent down to pick them up; the stub of a recently smoked cigarette, he sniffed it, menthol flavored, and a child's toy. A stuffed rabbit.

# CHAPTER FORTY FOUR

Morgan decided not to exit Ignatius Jackson's home the same way he had entered. He would leave via the front door. It was far more dignified than climbing over those railings again, though, any dignity he did have was superseded by the fact that his rear end protruded from his ripped trousers.

As soon as he opened the front door, he was met by two men, both wearing dark suits and sunglasses, both with stern looks on their faces and both with wires attached to their ears.

"And you are?" asked one of the men.

"Detective Morgan, Savannah PD. Who the hell are you?"

"That doesn't concern you," replied the man, flashing a badge in Morgan's face. "This property has been confiscated by the US Government. A matter of national security. All its contents remain inside. What is it have you there?" he asked, pointing to the files, cigarette butt, stuffed rabbit and shin bone that Morgan clutched to his chest."

"Evidence," replied Morgan.

"Hand them over," commanded the man.

"Okay, give me a second, let me lay them down, I am

about to drop them," answered the Detective. He returned into the house and placed everything he carried on the table that sat by Ignatius Jackson's front door. A second later he returned to the door and handed over three files, the stuffed toy, cigarette butt and the bone.

"Is this it, all you have, three files?" asked the dark suited man.

"Yes," lied Morgan, "and this bone, toy, and cigarette butt."

"Did you read them, the files?"

"No," and this time he told the truth, he hadn't, but he had wanted to.

"Okay, get out of here, you can keep the bone."

# CHAPTER FORTY FIVE

Peter Ferguson stood over the grave of his old friend. The burial had been a brief affair. There had been no other mourners in attendance, just him. He sighed as the last piece of earth was placed in the grave, and he nodded his appreciation to the grave digger as he departed the graveside, handing him a twenty dollar bill. Now, finally alone, Pete Ferguson mourned for Ignatius Jackson.

*They* had been good to their word; A burial at Arlington Cemetery for a man who had served his country valiantly; a hero, a highly decorated officer who not only had help defend the country as a soldier, but who had also been a loyal servant as a civilian. So what, thought Ferguson, the 'Organization' had deviated toward private contracts, so what if they had been 'guns for hire', the simple fact was that they were a tool, a device used by *them*, and irrelevant of the jobs not contracted by the government, they had been essential in protecting the country. *They* knew it, so, even though the 'Organization' was now finished, now closed, now nothing more than investigation that would eventually lead nowhere, *they* had understood.

*They* had ensured Pete Ferguson that Ignatius Jackson would never be linked to the 'Organization', *they* had promised Ferguson that Jackson's former home had been thoroughly 'cleaned'. There would be no link, no one who could connect the dots, and no one who could ever point any accusing finger at him.

Ignatius's home had been stripped of all documents, files, computers and printers. All equipment, including secure telephones, had been destroyed.

Of course, the 'Organization' would resurface, eventually, when the House Investigation by the Senate was over, once the dust had settled and all the leaks plugged. *They* needed the 'Organization', and *they* knew that *they* could not operate without them. Black Ops, 'unauthorized' killings, clandestine operations and deniable involvement were always needed, not just by America, but by her allies too. And the 'Organization' provided them, at a cost. Turning a blind eye to their 'private' business was something *they* had to accept.

There were, of course, many lose ends, many unanswered questions and just as many unasked. But Peter Ferguson's only concern at this time was his friend. He wondered if he had done the right thing; maybe Ignatius had wanted to be buried next to his wife in Savannah. However, that could have presented more problems, should some nosy cop, or determined Fed start asking too many questions. Ignatius's DNA could never be taken, only a Supreme Court judge could authorize the exhuming of a body interned at Arlington, and, not one of them would ever allow that. Peter Ferguson was confident of that.

Ignatius Jackson had broken many rules. He had contacted a contractor directly by sending his signed note to Doug Partridge warning him that his family was in danger. Somehow, someone had gotten a hold of a list naming contractors, indicating which 'jobs' they had carried out, against all protocols. The sad fact that Vladimir Derepaska's father, hell bent on avenging his son's death, had purchased Doug's information, and then murdered Doug's wife before taking his own life, had been 'unfortunate'. He shook his head. Gordonston. Of all the coincidences, of all the bad luck, that these so called 'civilized' people would resort to murder to settle their differences. Of course, it was over; all the files had been destroyed. None of the contracts would be fulfilled. Not that it mattered. How ironic, thought Ferguson, that two of those earmarked for death were already dead, but not at the hands of the 'Organization'.

Three contracts, all in the same neighborhood, one fulfilled by a contractor who actually lived in the same vicinity. It was, he guessed, fate. And, of course, his old friend Ignatius, the conductor of this crazy orchestra. Three. Just three. He had recalled that Ignatius had mentioned four contracts, but he must have been mistaken, because after the 'clean' only three files, containing details of those earmarked for death had been found. There was no way of double checking either, as all databases, all hard drives, all disk drives with any information pertaining to the 'Organization' had been wiped and destroyed. No, Ignatius had become confused, probably due to his sickness, there had only been three contracts, Billy Malphrus, Carla Zipp and Tom Hudd, and they were all now dead.

There was of course one other loose end he would have liked to have tied up, if he could. Doug Partridge. Wanted for the murder of Tom Hudd and his wife, as well as the kidnapping of his daughter. He doubted even *they* would find him. His name of course was false, even Pete Ferguson didn't know Doug Partridge's real name, and with multiple names and identities to rely on, the man was gone, a ghost, no doubt living in some far flung corner of the earth in retirement, and hopefully thankful for his freedom and the life of his daughter. But he was still a loose end, and worse, he was potentially a loose cannon. It would be simpler if he was dead. He was the only link; the only link left to Ignatius, and ultimately back to him. Maybe, once the organization reformed, regrouped and reinvented itself, he would make it a priority to find Doug Partridge and, for his own piece of mind, have him killed. The question was though, how do you kill a ghost?

He checked his watch. He had spent too much time thinking. He had responsibilities, and one of those responsibilities was sat in the back seat of his car. Before leaving Ignatius's graveside, he stood straight and saluted his old friend and then headed to his vehicle.

"Calm down," he said as he sat in the driver's seat. "Relax, Chalky, I am taking you home. A new home, with me. You will love it, boy, you will love it." Ferguson shifted his car into drive, and his new best friend sat in the back of the car, oblivious to where he was going, but still seemingly grieving the old man who had cared for him for so many years, and apparently happy that he had found a new master. Ferguson didn't know how long Chalky had, he was of course over 17 years old. He would spend his final days, though, spoiled and pampered, and Pete Ferguson had no intention of continually dyeing and bleaching the dog's fur, as Ignatius had. Chalky wagged his now darker tail, and barked.

# CHAPTER FORTY SIX

Cindy Mopper rarely ventured outside her home these days, unless it was to walk Paddy and Walter, or to shop for groceries. Sometimes she would venture into the park, usually at night, so no one would see her. She had, for all intents and purposes, become a recluse. She no longer played any role in the Gordonston Residents Association, she no longer produced the newsletter, and she was no longer the once energetic and efficient organizer of the Gordonston Book Club. The only person she ever encountered, and that was rarely, was Betty Jenkins, and only briefly, should Betty be walking Fuchsl at night. As for The Gordonston Ladies Dog Walking Club? It had ceased to be.

Cindy was a broken woman. Her life, she often thought, no longer had any meaning. Her only true friends were Paddy and Walter. Walter, Carla Zipp's bulldog, whom Cindy had not hesitated to adopt, poor confused Walter, who now lived with her and Paddy. Walter, like Cindy, had grieved for her old friend. Many were the times that Walter would sit crying, pining for his dead mistress. Often, during their nocturnal walks in the park, Walter would run off on his own, leaving Paddy confused, as he seemed, to Cindy at least, to be searching for Carla. Other times, while the three were walking towards the park, Walter would strain on his leash, apparently eager to return to his old home.

Lately though, it seemed that Walter was passing the grieving stage. He appeared to have settled in his new home with Cindy and Paddy, though, every so often, he would yelp with delight whenever he saw, from a distance, any woman who remotely resembled Carla.

Cindy had been through so much. Sometimes she would try her best to put it all behind her, to try her best to be strong, but the events of two months ago would inevitably destroy her thoughts, or desire, to see any sense in the unfortunate and horrific events that had occurred….

* * * * *

Cindy knew no one could hear her. As she cradled her dead friend in her arms, both Walter and Paddy whimpering, she cast a sad and pathetic figure as she slowly rocked on her kitchen floor.

She had eventually fallen asleep, her throat sore from shouting, her body exhausted and her emotions drained, that, all coupled with the sleeping pills she had taken, had led to Cindy not waking until the following morning.

It had been then, the day after, she had called the emergency services. An ambulance had arrived, closely followed by the police. The paramedics had pronounced Carla dead and had taken her body away, as Cindy tried to explain to the police what had happened, though, of course, she had no idea.

She had told the police all she knew. That her friend had been fine when she had last seen her, that Cindy had slept for three hours, as she was distraught and grieving for her poor nephew who had died earlier that day in a road accident. She told the police that she had found her friend lying on the kitchen floor and she had no idea, after repeated questions, if

Carla had any medical conditions or even allergies that could have triggered such a sudden death. The officers had asked her to accompany them to the police station, they had more questions, but after three hours, they had released her.

Cindy did not think that she would ever live through a worse day than the day both Billy and Carla died. But worse was to come. First there was Billy's funeral. Cindy organized everything, the casket, a burial plot, flowers and a memorial headstone. The only thing she could not organize were mourners. Not one soul, apart from Cindy herself, attended Billy's sad and lonely burial. His parents, Cindy's brother and his wife, simply did not show up for their son's burial. During a rather terse telephone conversation, Cindy had been informed that 'Billy had been dead to them for years'. Cindy could not believe it. Poor Billy, kind hearted, charitable Billy. She had argued with her brother, but he seemed not to care that his son was dead. He had even told Cindy that she was 'crazy' for even letting the boy stay with her, before he hung up.

Billy, it seemed, had very few friends, and even those friends he probably did have, Cindy had supposed, would be impossible to locate. His friends from the charities he worked for, his friends from college, she simply had no way of contacting them. She had, of course, called his old university, and explained that one of their alumni had passed away and that she would be hosting a funeral. Unfortunately, surely due to some incompetent administrator, the university could not find any trace of a Billy Malphrus ever graduating, let alone attending their school.

So, it was on a warm spring day that Billy had been buried, with a tearful Cindy the only attendee at his graveside.

Still in shock, and still grieving, not just for Billy but for Carla also, she had returned home, only to be greeted by two detectives, who had been waiting for her to return from Billy's funeral, sitting patiently in their car parked outside her home.

Cindy welcomed them into her home and offered them a

cold drink, which, to her surprise, they refused. Indeed their refusal to take anything Cindy offered them to consume was odd. They had both appeared to shout the word "No!" and made a point of shaking their heads and putting up their hands as if to stop a speeding bullet, not a slice of homemade apple pie and a glass of her self-made sweet tea.

"Mrs. Mopper," said the first detective, as he took a seat on Cindy's sofa, along with his colleague, who now both faced Cindy, who was on the easy chair in front of them.

"Cindy, please," replied Cindy, innocently and politely.

"Mrs. Mopper," continued the detective, ignoring Cindy's request to address her by her first name. "We have received the autopsy report from the Medical Examiner, regarding Mrs. Carla Zipp, and there are a few questions we would like to ask you." The detective stared at Cindy, his face stern. The second detective remained silent.

"It transpires that the cause of death of your friend was definitely poison."

"Poison?" said Cindy, visibly shocked by this revelation.

"Yes, she was poisoned," answered the detective. "Can you just once again, if you would, just run through the events of last week, the day your friend died?"

So Cindy did. She recounted accurately all she knew, including the half drank glass of lemonade; she told the exact same story she had told the attending officers and the detectives who had questioned her for three hours at the station, seven days earlier.

"This lemonade, the lemonade that your friend drank, who gave it to her?" asked the detective once Cindy had confirmed and not deviated from what the detectives already knew.

"No one," replied Cindy truthfully. "It was just in the refrigerator. I just told her to help herself to anything, while I rested. You have to realize it had been an awful day; my nephew had just died."

Both detectives indicated that they knew this, that they

knew all the circumstances surrounding the fateful day.

"Mrs. Mopper," said the second detective, who had remained silent up until this point, "where did this lemonade come from? Was it purchased, or did you make it yourself?"

Cindy held back a tear. It had been Billy who had made the lemonade, poor, generous, kind hearted Billy, who without prompting had thoughtfully made the refreshing and tasty drink for not just him, but for her also.

"No, it was my nephew, Billy. He had become rather good at it, making lemonade that is. He was such a dear boy, he had made it for me, and of course himself. In fact, it was the last thing he did, the last good thing that poor boy did, so thoughtful you see, such a good boy." Cindy was now crying, memories of Billy's endeavors of lemonade making flooding back; how he would spend hours making jugs of the stuff, just for them to share.

"Did you ever drink any of this lemonade?" asked the first detective.

"Yes, all the time, Billy and I both did. I am sorry but I don't understand."

"Did you drink any of the lemonade that was consumed by your friend on the day she died? Did you pour yourself a glass? From the same jug?" queried the first detective.

Cindy thought for a moment. Then shook her head. That morning Billy had prepared the jug of lemonade and had told her that it was fresh and cooling in the refrigerator. She had been busy. Walking Paddy in the park that morning with her friends from The Gordonston Ladies Dog Walking, she recalled that they had been engrossed in neighborhood gossip, mainly regarding the whereabouts of Tom Hudd, then she had gone to the bank to discuss her finances, or lack of them, as the case had been. She had returned home and had in fact wanted a glass. Indeed, she had poured herself some of the lemonade, but it hadn't chilled sufficiently for her liking yet, so she had poured it back into the jug, and had decided to wait an hour, until it was at a more palatable temperature. Of course, then had come news, the news of Billy's accident. So no, no she hadn't drunk any of Billy's homemade lemonade that day.

"Well, then, Cindy," said the first detective, whose initial apparent hostility and sternness had abated. "You are a very lucky woman, a very lucky woman indeed."

Cindy looked surprised.

"I can see you seem surprised," said the second detective.

"I am. I have no idea what you are talking about."

"The lemonade was poisoned, laced with rat poison actually. We believe that this poison was intended for you. We believe that your nephew, Billy Malphrus, had meant for you to drink it, just you, not your friend, and of course, how would he have known Mrs. Zipp would be here?"

Cindy shook her head. There must be some mistake. Why on earth would Billy want to kill her? He was one of the kindest, most honorable and trustworthy people she had known.

"No, there must be a mistake, I think you must be mistaken," protested Cindy. "What you are saying is ludicrous; that Billy wanted to poison me? Frankly it is the most bizarre thing I have ever heard."

Both detectives shook their heads. "Well, we have a search warrant; we would like to search your home. Do you have any rat poison?"

"No," said Cindy, "I certainly don't, but of course you are free to look. I have never purchased the stuff. I assure you, this house is spotless. I have a dog, two dogs now actually, so no rat would be crazy enough to show his face around here."

One of the detectives mumbled something, something that Cindy didn't quite catch, but was pretty sure he had whispered "apart from Malphrus" into the ear of his colleague, who had then stifled a smile.

While the detectives searched Cindy's house, including her garden shed, Cindy pondered their comments. Billy? Poison? It was just a crazy notion. There had to have been some sort of mistake. Cindy did not accompany the detectives in the search. She knew that there was no poison in the house.

Fifteen minutes later the officers returned to her living room, one of them carrying a canister emblazoned with the words "Rat Poison" in bold black letters.

"We found this in your shed," said the first detective. "It was hidden, well, at least it appeared hidden. Is this yours?" he said, lifting the container upwards, practically forcing it into Cindy's face.

Cindy shook her head. "No, I have never laid eyes on it before. Please tell me what is going on? I am confused. You are actually saying that Billy intended to poison me?"

The first detective once again spoke sternly. "It is a line of enquiry. However, there is another possibility, isn't there Mrs. Mopper?" The detective's return to addressing Cindy formally did not go unnoticed by her.

"Maybe you poisoned Mrs. Zipp?" said the detective. Cindy was unsure if this was a statement, a question or even an accusation.

"Was there any bad blood between you and the victim?" said the second detective.

Cindy froze. Her smile evaporated, her calm demeanor suddenly replaced by dread. She shifted uneasily in her chair. Oh my God, she thought, yes, there had been bad blood. She had paid an 'Organization' over $100,000 to have her friend killed. But that was ages ago. Since then she had tried her best, her very best, to cancel the contract on her friend, once she had realized that she had made a huge mistake. Once she had realized that Carla was not a threat to her and her aspirations of finding love with Elliott Miller. Could this 'Organization' somehow have orchestrated this? Could they have poisoned Carla? It had to be. There was no way, she thought, that Billy would ever harm her. The detectives had been playing with her. Surely they knew, surely they knew what she had done. But she didn't want Carla dead. She was her friend. Her best friend. It had all been a mistake.

"Well, Mrs. Mopper?" pushed the second detective, who had not failed to notice her discomfort.

"Absolutely not," replied Cindy, "she and I, Carla that is, were best friends. She came here to comfort me and support me that day. Why would I want to harm her? Ask anyone, ask anyone who lives in Gordonston, who lives in Savannah, we were friends. We had our own dog walking club. I would never harm her. What you are saying is totally impossible, and rather insulting. Should I be speaking to a lawyer? Are you accusing me of killing my friend?"

The detectives both shook their heads.

"Look, we understand how you are feeling; we just have to ask these questions. This is all quite a shock, I am sure," said the first detective. "We are going to take this," he indicated to the container of poison, "for analysis, and we also have a warrant to seize any computers you may have. It is just procedure. We will return them, or it, if you have only one. Our technical guys just need to do some checks."

Once again Cindy felt a wave of dread engulf her. Her computer. The same computer that no doubt contained traces of her internet searches, looking for ways to cancel a hit. Containing traces of her attempts to source out the 'Organization', containing all the evidence the police would need to charge her and convict for her the murder of her friend.

Cindy composed herself before speaking. "Yes, I have a computer."

"Then we shall be taking that with us," replied the detective.

The two detectives spent five minutes unplugging and disconnecting Cindy's computer. They handed her a receipt for both the poison and the computer and then left. They told her that they would be in touch; that they would be making further enquiries, and they advised Cindy she may want to retain the services of an attorney after all, and, if she was planning on leaving the country anytime soon, or even planning on taking a trip out of town, then not to. She was not under arrest, not yet anyway, they explained, but they were treating her as a suspect in the murder of Carla Zipp.

The following week seemed to be the longest of Cindy's life. She had two more funerals to attend; the funeral of Veronica Partridge, who had, was alleged, been murdered by her husband. Then there was the funeral of Tom Hudd, again, according to the rumors, most likely murdered by Doug Partridge. The new theory, which she had heard on the neighborhood grapevine, was that Partridge had discovered an affair between his wife and Tom. That he had killed first Tom, burying his body in the park, and he then returned to kill his cheating wife and had kidnapped their daughter, before most likely fleeing back to England. Both funerals, unlike Billy's, had been well attended. At least these sad events had proved to be a welcome distraction for her. Elliott had attended both burials; Cindy had spoken to him, and he had expressed his condolences for the loss of Billy, and of course the death of Carla. It was also the first time she had seen Kelly Hudd in over four months. She seemed to be returning to her old self. She had lost some of the weight that Cindy had heard she had gained. She was once again looking gorgeous, and seemed, though Cindy could have been mistaken, happy, which struck her as odd. She also noticed something else. Something that briefly worried her, but she had put that to the back of her mind. It was a crazy thought. She had been slightly upset, though, that while Cindy had expressed her condolences to Kelly regarding Tom's tragic death, Kelly had not even mentioned Cindy's loss.

Cindy did not retain an attorney. She would confess. She had decided that, once the police had done their traces or whatever they did to find out what people got up to on their computers, she would come clean. She would admit that she had hired the "Organization" to kill her friend; that she was indeed responsible for Carla's death, and that despite her attempts to stop any harm coming to Carla, she had failed to contact or even find any trace of the people she had hired to kill her. Obviously they had done it. They had somehow gotten into her home as she slept, added poison to Carla's drink and either forced her to drink it or, unwittingly, and without a clue that this 'Organization' had even entered the house, doctored her drink, and left as silently as they had arrived, without Carla's knowledge.

Cindy knew she was headed to jail. Probably for a long time. She had made arrangements for Paddy and Walter, for whom she now felt doubly responsible, to be 'adopted' by the only person she trusted, Elliott Miller.

Initially Elliott had been confused by Cindy's out of the blue and odd request that if anything happened to her, he would promise to take care of both Walter and Paddy. Elliott, being the good man Cindy knew he was, had of course said yes, but told her that he was a little perturbed by her request, and he asked if there was anything he could do to help her. Cindy had merely told him it was 'just in case', and luckily Elliott had not pursued his offer to help Cindy, nor ask more questions. It had felt odd, talking to Elliott, after all this had all been done for him, and he didn't even have a clue. The plotting, the hiring of killers and the eventual death of Carla; all done for love, Cindy's love for Elliott. Maybe he could have helped her; he was of course the Mayor, so possibly he could 'have a word' in someone's ear. Perhaps if Cindy told him that she had done this terrible thing for him, because she loved him, he would tell her that he loved her too, even tell her not to worry… and they could live happily ever after.

But it wasn't a fairy tale. This was real life, and of course death. There would be no happy ending. There was no magical fairy godmother waving a wand — just the cruel hand of destiny, wagging its finger in Cindy's face.

Cindy discreetly got her 'house' in order. She rewrote her will, donating everything she had not to The Gordonston Residents Association, but to a local animal shelter. She contacted a real estate attorney, and made him her proxy to sell her house. The day the police arrived, she was positive to arrest her, Cindy was busy cleaning her home, so that the next occupant, while she languished in prison, would move into a clean and respectful house. She even sent Walter and Paddy into the cellar, just in case there were rats living with her. But of course, there weren't, not anymore.

As before, it was the same two detectives who returned to her home, and as before, she welcomed them and offered them apple pie and sweet tea. Cindy would go with dignity, she would remain calm and be polite and she would respect what these police officers had to do. Though she expected them both to decline any offer of food or drink, she was quite surprised when both men accepted her offer of tea and homemade pie.

Once again the detectives asked Cindy to sit, and as before, she led them into her living room, but this time both detectives sat on the sofa, unlike before when the taller one had stood. Cindy took her seat, and was about to confess all, but before she could utter a word, the first detective, the shorter one, spoke.

"We have some rather disturbing news for you, Cindy."

"I know," replied Cindy, "I am ready."

The detectives looked at each other, seemingly confused as to what Cindy meant. Regardless, the shorter detective spoke again.

"Then what we are going to tell you isn't going to come as too much of a shock to you?"

"No, not at all, I kind of guess I deserve it. You know, I brought this all on myself."

Again the detectives looked confused.

"Well, there really is no need for you to blame yourself, Cindy, you are just as much a victim as anyone else," said the taller detective.

"Yes, Cindy, don't be so hard on yourself. You weren't to know," said the shorter one.

Cindy raised her hand before speaking. "No, I have been a

silly old woman, and I made a mistake, and it cost the life of my friend, something I deeply regret, something, detectives, I promise you I readily admit and am ashamed of."

The shorter detective stood from the sofa. So this was it. In any moment, thought Cindy, she would be handcuffed and led away. Something she accepted and deserved. As Cindy prepared to offer the detective her wrists, so he could more easily restrain her, he did something that surprised her.

"Cindy," said the detective as he approached her, gently touching her shoulder, "none of this is your fault. Please don't blame yourself. You are not responsible, and you should not burden yourself with unjustified guilt. You are an extremely brave woman, and we, both my colleague and I, are touched and frankly amazed at your attitude. Please don't blame yourself. You are not responsible for the actions of your nephew."

The detectives' words, for a moment at least, and from Cindy's perspective anyway, seemed to hang in the air. She eyed them both curiously, before she spoke.

"Sorry?" she said. "I seem to be slightly confused. Could you possibly explain what is actually going on?"

Which is what they did.

They had traced the poison found in Cindy's shed; it had been purchased locally, and a few days before Carla had unwittingly drunk the tasty, yet fatal, lemonade. It had been purchased from the Home Depot, which was located on Victory Drive. They, the police that was, had made enquiries. One man recalled a young man, a skinny man, who roughly met the description of Billy Malphrus, enquiring if rat poison could kill a human being, if, in the unfortunate event it was ever accidentally drank. The police then obtained the video surveillance tapes for that day from the store, and, as they had always suspected, there was video evidence of Billy Malphrus purchasing the rat poison.

Secondly, a thorough search of Cindy's computer hard drive had been conducted. It had transpired that there had been some recent searches conducted online, for the potency of rat poison and further searches pertaining to the use and dangers of other poisons which could be purchased at any hardware or even grocery store. One search, involving the actual replication of keystrokes, which had been retrieved from Cindy's computer, was 'how to poison your aunt', this was the technology the police possessed, they could trace everything. Furthermore, it seemed that the computer had also been used, many times, to compile internet searches for hit men, killers for hire and professional assassins. It was obvious to the police that Billy Malphrus had been plotting his aunt's murder for some time. How on earth he thought he would have gotten away with it, what with all the evidence on the computer, was simply mind boggling, the detectives told Cindy. Though they didn't say it to Cindy, they thought the man was a complete idiot, a buffoon, who had put no thought whatsoever into his plotting. He may as well have entered 'how to murder my Aunt Cindy' as an internet search, so compelling was the evidence.

Cindy sat open mouthed, she could not believe what she was hearing. "Billy? Billy tried to poison me? He wanted to kill me?" she asked the detectives. She was shaking and visibly upset.

"Yes," replied the taller detective, "and it would seem for some time. What was most worrying is that he was even considering hiring someone to kill you. He must have changed his mind, as although he searched online for hit men and such like, he never actually connected with any of them."

Cindy drew in a deep breath. Of course, the searches were her searches, trying to find the 'Organization' so she could cancel the contract on Carla. She recalled how the 'Organization' had advised her, the day she had actually hired them, how to completely remove all traces of her visiting their website from her hard drive. Obviously those instructions had been spot on, perfect, as apparently no link nor did trace appear linking the organization to her computer.

"We also have some more disturbing news, Cindy, about your nephew," said the shorter detective, his tone kind and soft.

Cindy was crying. Tears streamed down her face. Billy had planned to kill her. Why? Why would her loving nephew do such a thing? She didn't understand. He had no reason to harm her; she had been good to him, and he to her. The boy did charity work. It didn't make any sense. The fact that her friend had died, killed because she had drank poison meant for her, only added to her grief and confusion. Discovering she was the intended victim of Billy's poison-laden lemonade was more painful to bear than Billy's death. Surely, surely this was a mistake.

The shorter detective spoke again, not before offering Cindy a handkerchief to wipe her tears.

"It seems your nephew was not the person who you thought he was. We did some checking. You mentioned that he had recently traveled to Africa and India. Well, there is no record of these trips, no airline records, no trace of him ever returning from either place. Nor is there any trace of the charities he told you he worked for. In fact, it seems Billy was recently in Florida, Jacksonville, to be precise. He was working as a bus boy at a diner. We contacted the owner. He was fired from there just before he returned here, to Savannah, for stealing tips."

Cindy could not believe what she was hearing, but there was worse to come.

"We managed to access his e-mail account," said the taller detective, "and he had actually sent an e-mail, to a friend of his, explaining he was about to come into an inheritance, that he would be set for life, that soon he could return to Europe, and continue, how do I put this, I will use his exact words, 'ripping off and conning gullible women, just like that stupid lying bitch I told you about'. I am sorry, Cindy, but Billy was no saint; he was a con man."

Cindy was now rocking in her chair. She was in shock.

Billy must have seen her will, the will leaving everything to him. He must have planned this for money. Billy was a fraud. A liar. And he had sucked her in. She was devastated.

"We have spoken to his friend, who had no idea what your nephew was planning. He did tell us though what we already suspected, that Billy was nothing more than a con artist. His whole life, well the life he told you about, was a lie. We contacted Interpol, and it seems he had been traveling around Europe, most recently Paris, pretending to be a Count. Apparently he tricked several women into sleeping with him. We have no idea how many victims there have been as a result of your nephew's actions. However, his friend did tell us that the 'stupid lying bitch I told you about', apparently was from here, Savannah. He met her in Paris. He didn't mention any names that we could trace, but it seems your nephew did use your computer to search for a 'Gerry Gordonston'… any idea who that maybe?"

Cindy shook her head. She had no idea who Gerry Gordonston was; odd though, her surname was the same as the name of her neighborhood.

"Anyway," said the detective, "as Billy is dead and all the evidence points to him, then the case is closed. We are one hundred per cent certain his intended victim in his poisoning plan was you. Sadly, and rather unfortunately, it was your friend, Carla, who drank the poison intended for you."

Cindy did not speak. Her heart was broken. Billy. Billy had wanted her dead. Everything else the detective said washed over her. Her computer would be returned, since she was not a suspect, and they apologized for not only suspecting her, but for delivering the news they just had.

That was three months ago.

Cindy had of course taken her house off the market, and she had called Elliott and told him to forget about her comments regarding adopting Walter and Paddy. She had also assisted with the funeral of Carla Zipp, whose body had been released by the police into the custody of a man named

Gino, from Las Vegas. Cindy had helped organize the funeral service and wake for her friend, along with Gino, who had cried uncontrollably throughout the funeral, attended of course by Elliott. Apparently, it seemed, Gino and Carla were planning on getting together. She had already made plans to maybe leave Savannah and marry her old flame, the man whose love she had once rejected, but had now accepted.

Cindy Mopper had not gotten over Billy's betrayal. It had taken her months to come to terms with the fact that Billy was not the charitable and kind hearted nephew she had idolized. It had taken months for her to accept that he had planned her murder, despite neighbors' comments that they always thought he was a bad 'un. They had meant no harm, but their comments didn't help.

Eventually, Cindy's shock and disbelief turned to anger. Anger at herself for being hoodwinked and blinkered by Billy. Anger that she had believed every word he had told her. Anger that she had allowed herself to be so blinded by her own stupidity. Of course, her anger was abated slightly by relief. Relief that the police had no clue nor idea of her plot to have Carla killed. It wasn't, though, the only silver lining. Cindy wasn't sure, despite her earlier readiness to confess, if she was quite ready to spend the rest of her life in jail.

Now, as she sat alone in her kitchen, the kitchen where Carla had died and Billy had concocted his poisonous brew, she felt even more anger. Anger not generated by Billy Malphrus (may he rot in hell), but anger and even hatred for others. Cindy had become a bitter woman. Gone was her former compassion. Her happy demeanor evaporated; gone was her desire to please. No. The old Cindy had left the building and turned the lights out as she left. She had died the day she had found out about Billy's betrayal. The new Cindy was unrecognizable, not in looks, but in thought and mind.

She was filled with hate.

How could *he*? How could *he* have done it? Not Billy, though she did hate Billy, but not half as much as she despised *him*. She detested *him*, and she abhorred *her*. *They* disgusted her. If anyone deserved to die, it was *them*, most of all *him*. *He* had to pay. Cindy would, she had vowed, make *him* pay a high price for what *he* had done to her, and if that bitch got caught in her cross hairs as well, well, that would just be a bonus. The old Cindy Mopper was gone. No one walked over the new Cindy Mopper, no one would once again use her, dally with her emotions. She was sick of being the victim. No more, she vowed. No more.

And of course, there was that second silver lining, the money. Ironic really, she often thought, that it was actually Billy's death that had replenished her bank account, had enabled her to take her home off the market and had resulted in her once again being a woman of wealth. Taking out a life insurance policy on Billy, eight years ago, with the intention of giving him the accumulated cash value, once it had matured, had proven to be a most fortuitous decision.

# CHAPTER FORTY SEVEN

## ONE YEAR LATER

Savannah Chief of Police Sam Taylor knew that heads were going to roll. He knew that most likely he would be the one paying the price for the incompetency of his department. They had failed Veronica Partridge and they had failed Kelly Hudd. Instead of investigating Tom Hudd's disappearance, his department had ignored it. If they had done their job correctly, and a proper investigation had been carried out, let alone a search, they would have discovered his body. Maybe if they had, then Veronica Partridge would still be alive.

Taylor blamed one man for this debacle; Jeff Morgan He was an idiot; it was his incompetence that had led to all this, and yet, despite the Chief's attempts to fire and discipline him, he had been overridden by the Mayor. It was Morgan who should be taking responsibility, yet, to Taylor's frustration, no disciplinary action would be taken. Why the Mayor was protecting Morgan was not clear to Sam Taylor, but he knew that somehow either Morgan had something on the Mayor or the Mayor was a fool.

Chief Sam Tam Taylor would not give Elliott Miller the satisfaction of firing him. He would resign. Thirty years of loyal service, unblemished service, a position he loved, gone, due to the Mayor and his interfering. The investigations carried out not by his own department, but by the Georgia Bureau of Investigations, an investigation requested directly by the Mayor had concluded that Doug Partridge had killed both Tom Hudd and his wife after discovering an affair between them. It was bullshit. It didn't make sense. The investigation had been hijacked. His friends at the GBI had told him that other agencies, Federal Agencies, had gotten involved in their investigation. That someone high up, with even more clout than Savannah's Mayor and the State's Investigator's, had directed the investigation.

The conclusion of the final official investigation just didn't make sense. There was no proof Veronica Partridge and Tom Hudd had ever conducted an affair. Despite how ridiculous it was, it wasn't half as ridiculous as the theory initially presented by the fool Morgan. That Tom Hudd and Doug Partridge were gay lovers, and had run off together; that was preposterous. Somehow all the reports, every note written by Morgan and any information pertaining to his investigations, had vanished. Was his whole department working secretly for the Mayor? How many of his officers were involved in covering up for Morgan? What had Miller promised them?

In any event, he knew he would be the one taking the fall. He would jump, though, rather than be pushed. No matter how much it galled him, he could prove no wrongdoing.

But there were unanswered questions. Questions he wanted answers to, questions he would ask himself, once he resigned. But they could wait. He would carry out his own investigation, as a private citizen, despite the interference of the Mayor, GBI, FBI, CIA and God only knows who else was involved.

At least one investigation had been carried out correctly. At least they hadn't arrested poor Cindy Mopper. That would have been just too embarrassing, arresting the intended victim of a murder.

It also galled him immensely that his officers had been barred from even entering Ignatius Jackson's home. They had swooped, whoever they were, flashing badges, producing documents signed by high ranking government officials. By the time the SPD had gotten a chance to even get inside the old man's home, once Morgan had retrieved Tom Hudd's shin bone, and presented it to him, the backside of his trousers ripped, and his blue, rather grubby, underpants on show to everyone, the place was spotless. Nothing. No documents, no trace of any wrongdoing, even his body had gone. Whisked away to be buried at Arlington Cemetery by the 'men in black', as he now referred to the agents who had descended on Gordonston. No, there was more to this, and he wanted answers.

Then there was Derepaska. Why on earth would the father of a man, murdered years ago, fly thousands of miles just to commit suicide? For Pete's sake, it just didn't add up. Again, he had no answers. Once again his department had been told that the investigation was 'above their pay grade', and the 'men in black' had removed any trace that Stefan Derepaska had ever even been in Savannah. The old man's body had been repatriated, the gun he had used to shoot himself in the head mysteriously vanished and his home 'cleaned' by the same people who had 'cleaned' Jackson's house.

Sam Taylor was not a fool. Everything was connected. He didn't believe in coincidences. The ballistics report he had seen had shown no link between the rope that had killed Veronica Partridge and the rope which was now conveniently missing, discovered in Derepaska's home to kill himself. That was hogwash. Of course, it hadn't been his department who had carried out the forensic tests. No, another agency had done it, and he was sure it was utter fantasy. If no one else could put two and two together and come up with four, then he could. Derepaska had killed Veronica Partridge, he was sure of it, and *they* knew it. *They* also knew that somehow Ignatius Jackson was involved, but *they* had more power than him. *They* could do whatever *they* wanted.

One final thought that had kept him awake many times at night also nagged at him. Why were there no fingerprint records of Doug Partridge on file? Not even with immigration. Or Homeland Security? He knew that every foreigner entering the United States was fingerprinted, and he knew that anyone applying for a green card, which Partridge apparently had, needed to provide biometrics. Why was there no trace of this man? Not one government agency, not one police department, no one, had any record of him. Who was he? What was his connection to Jackson, to Hudd, to any on this?

Taylor threw down his pen and leaned back in his chair. He would beat Mayor Miller to it. He had already drafted his resignation letter. He could wait. But sooner or later he would get to the bottom of all this, and he would make them all pay for forcing him out. For making him the scapegoat for cover up after cover up. Of course, there was not much he could do to combat the other agencies. He knew that he would have no chance of ever exposing them, but he could expose one man. The one person who linked this all together. Somehow Elliott Miller was a part of this, maybe not the orchestrator, but he knew something, he was sure of it. He could wait, but he would investigate Miller, the 'Greatest Mayor Savannah had Ever Seen' and the man tipped to maybe one day become Governor of the State, and then, who knew? Could one day Miller run for even higher office? Not on Sam Taylor's watch. He would leave no stone unturned, there would be nothing about Elliott Miller he would not find out. He would have time; resigning he may be, but going quietly into the night? No. Elliott Miller was going to find himself in a world of pain, and that pain, was going to come from him.

# CHAPTER FORTY EIGHT

Detective Jeff Morgan knew he wasn't liked. He knew that his fellow officers did not respect him, that other detectives mocked him, not only behind his back, but to his face. They laughed when he arrived at work on his moped, they mocked his appearance, they even joked about his body odor, which was ridiculous, because he showered twice a week and went through a can of deodorant every month. He also knew that Chief Taylor had no confidence in his abilities, and that the Chief had twice recommended that he not receive a promotion. Far from being the department's 'best man', he knew he was regarded as the 'worse man'. He knew that he was regarded as incompetent.

That's why he had done it.

That's why he had taken the money; not that it was money that motivated him, it was the promises. The promises of promotion, of one day maybe even leading the department, the promise that, if things worked out, he would one day become the Chief.

The pleasure he would get, watching their faces as he rose

through the ranks, would be worth the minor indiscretion of accepting money from the Mayor. And it was minor, in fact it was, in his eyes, less than minor. It was nothing. Really, he should have kept his money and his promises, as there was really no case, but of course, when the Mayor offers you ten thousand dollars and the chance to prove his colleagues wrong, the chance to once and for all hush their derogatory comments, their jokes and their ridicule, and to become head of the department, what else could he say apart from yes?

When Elliott Miller had approached him with a very simple request, backed up by the offer of money and promises of promotion, he had seen no problem at all in becoming the Mayor's inside man and eyes and ears of the department and of course destroying all his notes regarding the disappearance of Tom Hudd, including the fact that the Mayor had accompanied Hudd's wife when she made the initial report. Not that that was an issue anyway. The man had obviously left his wife; she had been cheating and he found out, and then, of course, Tom Hudd had been cheating with Veronica Partridge, and when Doug Partridge found out, he first killed Hudd, and then returned to strangle his wife. His initial theory, of the two men being lovers, hadn't been too far from the truth; it was just a different Partridge who was Tom Hudd's secret lover.

He had not asked the Mayor why he had wanted a lax investigation, why he had not wanted a search carried out nor what his interest in the disappearance in Tom Hudd was. It didn't matter. As far as he was concerned, there had been no need for any search, nor real investigation. That was then; however, that was before the events of last year. Before that dog had dug up Tom Hudd's body in the park, before the autopsy had shown he had been shot through the head, before Doug Partridge had killed his wife, before that old man had shot himself, before he had discovered the body of Ignatius Jackson, rotting in his bed, before he had discovered that office.

He had been sure questions would be asked, questions as to why he had not investigated the case in more detail, why he had not at least made some enquires regarding Doug Partridge's disappearance, why he had not searched for Tom Hudd. The Chief had told him that things were now out of his hands, that the Feds were involved, and that even the CIA were asking for more details. Morgan knew he had messed up. His only hope now was that there would be no trace of any monies passing between him and the Mayor; that no one ever discovered their little arrangement. Of course, no one would, he was sure. He was sure the Mayor was not going to jeopardize himself, that there was no way he would implicate himself in a bribery scandal. And he had been right. All blame had shifted from him; somehow the Mayor had protected him, as he had promised he would. There was now even talk of promotion, being the 'Mayor's man' had its advantages.

However, Jeff Morgan was not a totally stupid man. He had taken a precaution. He had something, something that he knew he should have left in that office, that he should have handed over to the two agents when he was leaving Ignatius Jackson's home, but he had taken it, before the FBI, CIA and God only knew who else had descended on the old man's home. He had the file. The file on Elliott Miller. It was, he guessed, his insurance policy, should the Mayor decide to come clean, should the Mayor betray him, and of course, should the Mayor decide not to honor his promise of promotion. Yes, he had the file, no one had seen it apart from him, and though he didn't know just what involvement or connection Elliott Miller had in the events of the last week, at least he had something, something to preserve himself, just in case. He had dallied with the thought of maybe warning the Mayor, warning him that this now defunct "Organization" had a contract out on him, and that possibly someone wanted him dead, just as someone had wanted Billy Malphrus, Carla Zipp and Tom Hudd dead. He had thought maybe he should warn him, but, for Jeff Morgan, self-preservation came first.

# CHAPTER FORTY NINE

"Is there anything else I can do for you before I leave?" asked Betty Jenkins as she finally finished wiping the dishes and putting them on the draining board.

"No, nothing else. Thank you, Betty, you run along; I know you are busy."

"Okay, I will be back tomorrow morning, at nine, as usual."

"Yes, dear, you run along; I am fine."

Betty Jenkins put on her coat and headed towards the door.

"Don't forget your keys, Betty, you always forget your car keys."

"I've got them," replied Betty as she produced her car keys from her pocket.

"Drive carefully," said Heidi Launer, as she took a sip of sweet tea, "and see you tomorrow."

Heidi Launer smiled sweetly as she watched Betty leave. The poor woman had been a nervous wreck after the tragic accident a year ago. It was of course, not her fault, and in fact the police had concluded that Billy Malphrus was to blame entirely for his own death. Running into traffic like he had. Silly boy, thought Heidi, but, he had deserved it. He was a bad one, she had known that from the moment she had lain her eyes on him. It was Cindy she felt sorry for. The poor woman. What that boy had done to her, or at least tried to do. Never mind the fact that he poisoned poor Carla by mistake. Good riddance to bad rubbish, thought Heidi as she took another sip of tea.

She closed her eyes. One year ago. It only seemed like yesterday….

*****

Click. Nothing. She pressed the trigger again. Click. No bang, no pain, nothing. Just the feeling of cold steel against her forehead. Heidi removed the Luger from her head and sat down. The darn thing wasn't working. Maybe it had never worked, or maybe it was because it was over seventy five years old and possibly never even fired before. One thing was for sure though. She wasn't dead.

There must be another way, she thought, once satisfied that her most prized possession in the world would not end her life, maybe she would hang herself? No. Hanging was for traitors and the defeated. She was neither. As she pondered how best to end her life, Fucshl whimpered. She turned to face her loyal pooch. Maybe he could sense that something was wrong? Heidi suddenly realized that she had made no provision for her dog. Who would look after him? What would become of him? Betty Jenkins didn't much care for dogs, and she doubted Betty would take him. She needed more time to plan for what would become of Fuchsl. If the wretched Luger worked, she could just shoot him, then herself, but she could hardly hang a dog, or smother him, or even drown him in the bathtub. Fuchsl was a large dog, and there was no way he would comply with being drowned. She would sleep on it, lock all the doors and windows, set her alarm, and sleep with a knife besides her bed, should Stefan try and kill her in her sleep.

The following morning she had woken at eight, late for her, but she had not slept well, and she would have probably slept longer if hadn't been for the sound of sirens; lots of them. They were close. In the neighborhood. She put on her slippers, covered her night clothes with a dressing gown and called Fuchsl. She placed his leash on him and headed outside to see what the commotion was, thoughts of imminent suicide temporarily abated, as well as thoughts of the soon-to-come revelation as to her true identity.

She had never seen so much police activity. Everywhere she looked there was blue and red flashing lights. With Fuchsl at her side she ventured onto the street, she was not going to die before knowing what the heck was going on.

"Young man," she shouted, "young man, please tell me what is going on? How is a lady, and her dog, meant to sleep with all this commotion going on?"

The young police officer smiled. A nosy old biddy. He walked towards Heidi and Fuchsl, who seemed to be just as mesmerized by the all the flashing lights as Heidi was.

"Well, where do I start?" said the officer.

Heidi put on her best false smile. "From the beginning is usually best."

"Well, I might as well tell you, seeing as though the press are already here. I am afraid there has been a murder. Some woman on Kinzie Avenue. Partridge, Veronica. Do you know her?"

"Vaguely," replied Heidi.

"Well, we are looking for her husband, and her daughter, not saying he did it, but if you see him, then let us know."

"Oh, I know him. Lazy man, good for nothing scruffy 'stay at home dad'. I haven't seen him for months. I thought he left her?"

The officer nodded. "Just keep your eyes open. Not saying it is him, but we would like to speak to him."

Heidi nodded. Indicating that if she set eyes on the man

she would call the police immediately. Not that she would. She would be dead herself soon, now that her curiosity had been served. Maybe she would just lie in the bath, drink a bottle of Schnapps and fall asleep. She had heard that drowning was quite a pleasant and painless death.

The police officer turned to leave, to return to join in the hunt for Doug Partridge, then he turned back to face Heidi.

"Oh, and something else. I guess you will find out anyway, but maybe you could help."

"Help?" asked Heidi. "With what?"

"Did you know a man named Stefan? He lives on Henry Street? Foreign fellow, apparently only been living here for a few weeks."

Heidi shuddered, but maintained her false decorum and smile.

"No," she lied, "I have never heard of him, nor met him, who is he?"

"Who was he, would be a better question," said the officer shaking his head. "He was just found in his house. Shot himself in the head. Dead, obviously, just wondered if you knew him. Seems he may not be, or wasn't, who he said he was. Anyway, if you think of anything, just call us."

Heidi stood open mouthed as she watched the young policeman return to the sidewalk. She pulled on Fuchsl's leash and led him back into her house. She was shaking. What had she nearly done? She had nearly shot herself for no reason. Stefan probably wasn't even his real name. She had made a mistake. There was no danger. Even if there had been, it was gone now. She stared at the Luger, still on her kitchen table. How close had she come to ending her own life? She sat down, unleashing Fuchsl who headed for his bed. Later she would get all the gossip, from Cindy and Carla, when they met for their dog walking club, in the meantime, she would have a stiff drink, just to settle her nerves….

*****

One year ago. Heidi opened her eyes. Of course she

hadn't gossiped that morning. The morning had brought even more shocking news. She still missed Carla. Poisoned. The poor woman. And of course Cindy. How dreadful, how utterly dreadful.

Heidi stood and headed upstairs. Fuchsl followed her. Taking her key that now lived on a chain around her neck, she unlocked the door and entered her private sanctuary. Her sanctuary filled with memories and relics of the past. She passed the cabinet that housed her Luger, the malfunctioning Luger, which had saved her life. She walked slowly, but purposefully towards the window, the window that overlooked the garden of her neighbor, Elliott Miller.

Heidi's face hardened, and with a look of pure hatred she continued to stare at the big white house. She had never heard why they hadn't killed him. Never found out why her contract to have the man she despised above all others had never been fulfilled. Her incompetent son Stephen, who had organized everything, had been told by the criminals he defended to just forget it. That it was best if he didn't ask too many questions.

Heidi sneered. It wasn't over. Sooner or later she would have vengeance. Elliott Miller was living on borrowed time. There was more than one way, she thought, to skin a cat. One day, one day soon, she would make him pay. Mayor or no Mayor, if it was the last thing she did, she was still determined to kill Elliott Miller.

# CHAPTER FIFTY

Betty Jenkins was an educated woman. The fact she may clean and cook for Heidi Launder didn't mean she was just a cleaner. She kept house for Heidi out of necessity. She needed an income, she needed to work. Like Heidi she was a widow, but unlike Heidi, Cindy and Carla, whose husbands had been replaced with a large life insurance policy and financial security, she had struggled, and as a one parent family and single mother it had been hard. She had taken in laundry, cleaned, and worked her fingers to the bone to provide a decent life and education for her son, Anthony.

She had been the proudest woman in the world when he was accepted into the air force academy; she had been even prouder when he graduated as a fighter pilot. He promised his mother that her days of cleaning and cooking for rich widows would soon be a thing of the past. That, just around the corner, there was a better life waiting for her.

He had been a good son. Betty, as well as producing the best fried chicken in Savannah and being able to clean a three story house; impeccably in less than four hours, was also a very intuitive woman. She had met Billy Malphrus only once, and had taken an instant dislike to him. She found him 'shifty' and guessed he was nothing more than a chancer, a 'grifter', with only one thing on his mind, ripping folks off for their money. She had shed no tears for Billy Malphrus, and the only guilt she felt after the accident was the damaged caused to her driving instructor's car.

Carla Zipp she had found shallow and false. Self-centered and man hungry, no doubt she had been a nasty little tramp in her day, maybe even worse, quite possibly a whore. She had flaunted herself, unashamedly. Once again, Betty had not mourned for her either.

Cindy Mopper was a sheep. A follower who would rather believe a lie than contemplate the truth. Betty found her to be pathetic. Continually gossiping, getting into everyone's business, a real busybody. The fact she had become obsessed with Elliott Miller made her even more ridiculous in Betty's eyes. Have some respect, woman, she thought, as she would listen to Heidi's reports from her dog walking sessions.

As for employer, Heidi, Betty knew that she was a self-important bully. Demanding, often rude and domineering. She had heard her on numerous occasions screaming at the top of her voice. She also knew Heidi had secrets. There was only one reason she had paid for Betty's driving lessons, and that was because she wanted Betty to be her chauffeur. As for the car, while she had been told by Heidi she could use it, whenever she wanted, Heidi would never let her use it to go out of town, to visit her distant relatives, or maybe even drive her friends to church, nor visit the graves of her loved ones, one buried so far away, in Arlington Cemetery.

Betty Jenkins had read somewhere that one in twenty five Americans were sociopaths. That four per cent of the adult population of the United States were impervious to the bonds of love and cared about nothing but power over others and themselves. That they had no conscience, that they were self-serving, selfish and had one priority, themselves.

Betty Jenkins had no doubt that the majority of people whom she encountered in Gordonston were sociopaths. They were motivated by greed, by creating their associations and groups, with the sole intention of excluding others, showed Betty that they had a predisposition for trying to have power over others. For all its manicured lawns and the falseness of the good mornings and good afternoons, the upright citizens of this so called 'upscale neighborhood' repulsed her. She harbored not a hint of respect for those who undoubtedly held no respect for her. She wasn't even allowed in the park, unless, on the odd occasion, she was walking Fuchsl.

Those people did not know what it was to struggle, to have something to worry about other than their gardens, which book to choose next for the book club meeting or whose dog was pooping in the park.

And while she had received nothing from her dead husband, she had received something from her dead son. Every day she cleaned the medal that lay draped over his photograph — the medal the Air force had given her, the medal they had given her to replace her son.

# CHAPTER FIFTY ONE

Elliott Miller was a happy man. His first year in office had been nothing but an unmitigated success. The people of Savannah loved their Mayor, and he had the highest approval ratings of any holder of the office. Tourism was up and crime was down. The economy was booming, and visitors were flocking to the Hostess City in droves. His urban redevelopment programs had turned former unsavory areas of the city into attractive and crime-free zones. He had appointed a new city manager who had shared Elliott's vision of growth and rebuilding. There was even talk of Elliott maybe running for an even higher office in the future, maybe as a senator or even as Governor of the state.

Of course, there had been the events in Gordonston that had overshadowed his first month in office. The murders of Tom Hudd, Veronica Partridge and his friend, Carla Zipp. Briefly these events had been big news, but like anything else, as time passed, the sensation and interest had died down.

Naturally, Elliott and the Savannah Police Department had attempted to investigate these crimes. The investigation, though, had been hijacked by powers far more potent than Elliott. The final outcome of the so called investigation had led to one suspect – Doug Partridge. The 'investigation' had concluded that Doug Partridge had killed first Tom Hudd and then later his wife after discovering an affair between the two. Partridge had then abducted his own child. It was supposed that Partridge was now in hiding, probably abroad, living with his daughter. All leads, though, had failed to find him, and despite a so called 'search' for the killer, it was assumed he would one day slip up, and it would only be a matter of time before he was caught; he could not hide forever.

Elliott Miller, though, knew the truth. Doug Partridge was a ghost, he did not exist, and the man whom the world knew as Doug Partridge would not slip up, would not reveal himself. He was gone; a spook in the night. What his name really was, was not important. Elliott Miller knew if he wanted to further his ambitions as a politician, then he would be wise to keep his knowledge to himself. Knowledge gained by his spies not only within the Savannah Police Department, but his paid contacts at the GBI and his new connections, high up in the government, connections who had seemingly spotted Elliott's political potential of one day attaining a role that could see him running for *the* office. Of course, it had proven beneficial for him to go along with the findings of the investigation. Savannah had received extra government grants that had enabled Elliott's projects for the city to flourish. The Savannah Police Department, still led by Sam Taylor, for now at least, had had its budget increased. He had also insured that his 'mole', Jeff Morgan, remained well-protected, in fact Elliott was going to suggest that he receive a promotion. Money did indeed talk, but it also ensured silence.

Elliott poured himself another glass of scotch as he sat back in his chair, Biscuits and Grits sleeping soundly at his feet and the new addition to his canine family asleep on his bed.

A house full of dogs, Elliott smiled to himself, Thelma

would have loved this; she would have been in her element, spoiling them, spending hours in the park opposite with her friends and fellow dog walkers. Elliott suddenly felt a tinge of sadness, of course, though, her friends were no longer all here. Thelma would have been heartbroken about the tragic death of Carla Zipp, and of course the plight of poor Cindy Mopper.

Elliott had only seen Cindy twice during the past year, since the day she had asked him to care for Walter and Paddy, should anything happen to her, and each time, since then, he had encountered her, she had ignored him, turning in the other direction and deliberately avoiding any contact with him. It was rumored that she walked her dog during the early hours of the morning, or late at night, alone in the park. It was also rumored that she would spend hours sitting at the picnic table that had once been the domain of The Gordonston Ladies Dog Walking Club, staring blankly in the direction of Elliott's home. She had also not responded to his invitation, which he found not only rude, but slightly strange.

Elliott's thoughts were interrupted by footsteps, footsteps coming down the stairs.

"Are you coming to bed or not?" asked his wife.

Elliott smiled. This was why he was happiest. His wife. His beautiful young wife whom he had married three months ago.

"Yes, just give me a minute," he smiled.

"Did you let the dogs out?" asked his wife.

"Yes, Biscuits and Grits just sniffed around, like they always do."

"Those dogs, you know you pamper them?

"And you don't pamper your dog?" he said smiling.

He grinned and looked at the two sleeping dogs. Dogs, he thought, they just want love, just want to play, to be fed, to be respected. In some sense maybe he was like a dog; he needed love, craved respect and of course liked to be fed. As for playing, well, he had a beautiful wife and of course they played.

"And where is my baby?" asked his wife as she scanned the living room.

"Oh, he is curled up in the kitchen. You know Shmitty, he likes his privacy. What is he anyway, a yellow Labrador or a yellow Retriever, or a golden Labrador or is he a golden Retriever?"

Kelly Miller smiled at her husband. "He's a Labrador retriever, but for arguments sake, let's just say he is a Labrador, don't you know the difference? Come on, honey, let's go to bed, it's late."

Elliott Miller had indeed proven to be Kelly Hudd's knight in shining armor, as he had always planned. It had been he who had insisted she be released from the hospital, the day after Billy had died, after she had been admitted to a psychiatric wing. It had been Elliott who had comforted her during Tom's funeral and it had been his shoulder she had cried on, once it had been revealed her husband had been screwing Veronica Partridge. And of course, it had been Elliott who had paid for her expensive psychiatric treatment. He had hired the best doctors and therapists for her, and paid for everything. The day he told Kelly that it was he who had been keeping up with her mortgage payments, that her house was not in foreclosure, she had not only hugged him, but for the first time kissed him. On the lips.

Kelly had fallen in love with Elliott Miller. Of course he was older than she was, of course his looks and body could never compete with Tom, but Kelly was not the same Kelly she had been. She wanted a man she could trust, a man who loved her, who cared for her, who adored her. And Elliott Miller was that man. He also had power; he was the Mayor, he was also wealthy. In Kelly's mind, he was the perfect replacement for Tom.

# CHAPTER FIFTY TWO

As Heidi Launer stared out of her window towards Elliott Miller's home, Cindy Mopper stood in the park, also staring at the big white house. As Walter and Paddy played in the darkness, enjoying the park, exploring and chasing squirrels, she just stared.

They had invited her to their wedding, but she had feigned an excuse. She would not attend. She would not give him the satisfaction. Elliott Miller had broken her heart, and she blamed him for everything. He may be the Mayor, he may be popular, but to her he was scum. She despised him now. Everywhere he went he had a smile on his face. They said he was a political genius, his popularity sky high, that this was just the beginning, that one day who knew where Elliott Miller could end up?

It should have been her by his side. It should have been her who accompanied him to social gatherings and on official business; she would have been perfect. Not that bitch. Not that stupid, idiotic, pathetic, but beautiful woman who a few months ago had become Mrs. Miller.

Thelma would be turning in her grave if she could see what her husband was doing. Thelma had told her many times, many, many times that Cindy would be ideal for Elliott. It was Thelma's wish, she just knew it, that one day Elliott would marry Cindy.

As Walter and Paddy played in the park and Cindy continued staring at Elliott and Kelly Miller's home, she didn't notice the car that pulled up to the curb. She was too engrossed in her thoughts of revenge, hatred and anger, all directed at Elliott and Kelly Miller, to register its arrival, let alone its departure, one minute later.

# CHAPTER FIFTY THREE

The car crept slowly into Gordonston, the avenues, only lit from streetlights added to the feeling of emptiness. He checked the time; it was midnight. He drove slowly, passing his former home as he toured his old neighborhood. He considered stopping, parking the car and maybe looking through the windows to see what had become of the place. A for sale sign had been placed in the front yard. There was no mortgage on the property and the home would now have formed part of his dead wife's estate. By rights that money should go to Katie, but how that could transpire he did not know. Instead of stopping he drove on, cruising the avenues and streets he used to call home.

Once again he considered stopping as he circled the park. So many memories, so many regrets. He noticed another for sale sign, this time on the front yard of the former home of Ignatius Jackson; the Director. He had always liked the old man and wished he had got to know him better. He could only guess, by the state of the overgrown lawn, that that home was also now empty. He had seen Ignatius's body, the night he had entered his house, searching for clues as to who may have killed his wife. He had not removed anything, but he had seen the files on Carla Zipp, Tom Hudd, Billy Malprhus and Elliott Miller. He wondered, albeit briefly, what had become of the man's dog; he guessed that the old fella had probably also died. He knew he owed Ignatius Jackson gratitude, though; if only he had acted sooner, returned to Savannah just one day earlier....

As he continued his navigation of the neighborhood, he suddenly spotted movement in the park. A woman was sat at the picnic table, the picnic table that had once been the domain of those petty old ladies. This time he put the car in park and, sure that he could not be seen, tried to get a better view of the solitary figure, just staring at the large white house opposite.

It was Cindy. As he stared over towards her, he could see that she was crying. He could see that she seemed disheveled. He noticed movement and saw that she was not alone; her dog, Paddy, the Irish setter was off his leash and exploring the nocturnal delights of the park, followed closely by Walter. Five minutes passed and she eventually stood, called for her dogs, who immediately yielded to their mistress' voice and together they exited the park. Once he was sure she had left the park, he shifted his car into drive and headed in an anti-clockwise direction, turning left on Goebel Avenue, then left again on Park Avenue before taking another left and eventually parking his car outside the large white house. All was quiet; no one stirred within the house, and he was satisfied that no one had seen his arrival or heard his vehicle. He glanced into his review mirror and stared at his reflection. His hair was long, over his shoulders, and his beard covered most of his face. Lately, when looking at his reflection, he did not recognize himself, and he was sure no one else would. It was hard to believe that at one time he had been Doug Partridge, father, husband, and neighbor — and not wanted for two murders. Doug Partridge was gone, but the memories of Doug Partridge still lived in his mind. His wife, his murdered wife, his daughter, his perfect daughter, now living with his parents, living with a new name, a new identity and, as far as he was concerned, and of course most importantly, safe.

He had vowed that this would be his last job. He didn't need the money, he didn't want it. His greed had already cost the life of his wife and very nearly his daughter. There had been enough killing. He more than anyone else knew that, but Elliott Miller had something to do with Veronica's death, he was sure of it. Why, of the four files he had seen on the Director's desk, was Elliott Miller the last man standing? Had he done a deal with the 'Organization'? Was it possible he had been the one who had killed Veronica and not Derepaska?

He would wait though, lie low in Savannah, and assume a new identity, until it was time. He could afford no slip up, afford no mistakes, he needed to find out what Elliott Miller knew about Veronica's death, and he would kill him, if he had to, if he didn't get the answers he wanted.

The man once known as Doug Partridge stared at the white house, and delved into his pocket and retrieved a packet of menthol cigarettes. He lit one and sucked in the menthol flavored smoke before switching on his car's ignition and slowly driving away, the park to his left, the park that once had been the stomping ground of The Gordonston Ladies Dog Walking Club.

# ABOUT THE AUTHER

The life of Duncan Whitehead, winner of the 2013 and 2014 Reader's Favorite International Book Award for Humor and Gold Medalist, is as quirky as his works. Born in 1967, he served in the Royal Navy in embassies across South America and was an amateur boxer. He worked as a purser on some of the world's largest super yachts and visited many exotic places. He's also an instructor of English as a foreign language, fluent in Spanish, and a children's soccer coach.

Duncan retired to Savannah, Georgia, to pursue his passion—writing. Mindful that we all harbor secrets and inspired by the locale's odd characters, he wrote *The Gordonston Ladies Walking Club*, a dark comedic mystery.

In 2011, Duncan spent six months in Brazil before settling in Fort Lauderdale, Florida. His interests include cooking, the Israeli self-defense art of Krav Maga, and Dim-Mak, a pressure-point martial art.

He has written over two thousand comedy news articles for US and UK websites, and *The Reluctant Jesus*, an award winning comedic novel set in Manhattan.

His latest novel, *Unleashed*, the highly anticipated sequel to *The Gordonston Ladies Walking Club* is his fourth book.

# TABLE OF CONTENTS

Printed in Great Britain
by Amazon